Nancy Graham

AESTHETICS IN SCOTLAND

Aesthetics in Scotland

By HUGH MACDIARMID
Edited & Introduced By ALAN BOLD

MAINSTREAM PUBLISHING

This first edition published by
MAINSTREAM PUBLISHING COMPANY
(EDINBURGH) LTD.
25a South West Thistle Street Lane
Edinburgh EH2 1EW

ISBN 0 906391 60 1

The Publishers gratefully acknowledge financial assistance from the Scottish Arts Council in production of this volume.

For use of illustrations, the editor and the publishers gratefully acknowledge the following:

National Galleries of Scotland for Raeburn's "Macdonell of Glengarry", Allan Ramsay's "The Painter's Wife" and Robert Colquhoun's "The Dubliners"; Mary Johnstone for William Johnstone's "Water Colour, 1931"; Margaret McCance for William McCance's "From another window in Thrums"; Robert Crozier for his "Men in Pub, 1971"; John Bellany for his "Self-Portrait with Owl Mask"; and Alexander Moffat for his "Summer Evening 1974".

Jacket design by James Hutcheson
Typeset in 12/14pt Perpetua by
Hewer Text Composition Services, Edinburgh
Printed and bound by Clark Constable (1982) Ltd., Edinburgh

Contents

Introduction

THE first appearance in print of an unpublished work by Hugh MacDiarmid (1892–1978)—a man recognised as one of Scotland's greatest writers and the poetic peer of Yeats, Pound, Neruda—can be regarded as an important literary event in its own right. What makes this work, *Aesthetics in Scotland*, especially remarkable is that in it MacDiarmid explores in detail a philosophical area not normally associated with him. Here, for the first time, MacDiarmid is seen to articulate at length those aesthetic principles that illuminated his entire career.

Aesthetics in Scotland was written in 1950, at a transitional time, for that year MacDiarmid moved from Glasgow (where he had worked as a precision fitter during wartime) to return to his rural roots. The Duke of Hamilton, whose brother knew MacDiarmid through a mutual interest in the Saltire Society, offered the poet a five-apartment outhouse at his home—Dungavel House, Strathaven, Lanarkshire. There, in September 1950, MacDiarmid completed *Aesthetics in Scotland*; shortly afterwards the National Coal Board bought the Duke's property and so MacDiarmid had to find another home (which he did when he settled, for the rest of his life, in Brownsbank Cottage near Biggar, Lanarkshire).

As he wrote *Aesthetics in Scotland* in the beautiful environment at Dungavel, the "singer after the fashion/Of my people—a poet of passion" was in one of his valedictory moods and ready to assess the aesthetic status of Scotland. In the process he pronounced on problems still to be resolved so the essay is both retrospective and radical in tone. It is also thematically alive to the cultural issues that continue to concern Scotland.

When Hugh MacDiarmid (or C. M. Grieve to give him the real name he still wrote under at the time) announced the advent of a Scottish Literary Renaissance in 1923 he insisted on the modernist nature of the enterprise. Writing in *The Scottish Chapbook* (February 1923) he opposed the sentimentality of some Scots as "belonging to a type of life that has passed and cannot return [as] a sort of museum department of our consciousness". MacDiarmid, who wanted to encourage "the experimental exploitation of the unexplored possibilities of Vernacular expression", held up James Joyce as a shining artistic example to his fellow Celts. Scots were no longer to see themselves as others saw them but to wake up to new possibilities. The narrative gist of MacDiarmid's masterpiece, *A Drunk Man Looks at the Thistle*, suggests that the spirit-besotted Scot can be reborn in a spiritual dimension. In a letter of 1 November 1926 to Pittendrigh MacGillivray MacDiarmid attempted an Epilogue in which the Drunk Man sees the new light:

> And yet gin I could fa' asleep
> To wauken here at fresh o' morn
> Hoo bonnie micht this thistle seem
> Wi' jinglin' dew on ilka thorn!

In *Aesthetics in Scotland* MacDiarmid himself sees Scotland in an aesthetically bright light.

It was always MacDiarmid's hope that the other arts would evolve to maturity in Scotland as the aims of the Scottish Literary Renaissance were implemented. At Langholm Academy, MacDiarmid's English teacher had been Francis George Scott who influenced and encouraged him. Later MacDiarmid supplied Scott with lyrics for his majestically melodic song-settings, dedicated *A Drunk Man Looks at the Thistle* to him, and promoted him as the saviour of Scottish music in (for instance) *Francis George Scott: An Essay on the Occasion of his Seventy-fifth Birthday* (1955). MacDiarmid was also anxious to encourage the visual arts in Scotland and drew on his close friendship with the painters William Johnstone and William McCance in extending his knowledge of the subject. Johnstone, who studied under André L'Hôte in the Paris of the 1920s, was one of the first important Scottish artists to exploit the emotional possibilities of abstraction. McCance settled in London in 1919 and began to adapt the Vorticist idiom to his own ends. He was also art critic of *The Spectator* from 1923 to 1926 and so in a position to enunciate the artistic gospel according to Wyndham Lewis (who was, with Joyce and Eliot and Pound, one of the modernist "men of 1914").

MacDiarmid's interest in visual art was also stimulated by his friendship with the late John Tonge to whom MacDiarmid (partly) dedicated his *In Memoriam James Joyce* (1955). Tonge was closely associated with J. H. Whyte's magazine *The Modern Scot* which adhered to modernist tenets. Subsequently Tonge was one of the most enthusiastic advocates of the work of the painters Robert Colquhoun and Robert McBryde, men well-known to MacDiarmid as untypical Scots with painterly flair and personal panache. In his later years Tonge became a familiar figure in the literary pubs of Edinburgh's Rose Street. His anecdotal talk about cultural affairs was erudite and entertaining and he conveyed the sheer aesthetic excitement of visual art. MacDiarmid's long essay on aesthetics begins, appropriately enough, with a tribute to John Tonge.

From the time he edited the annual poetry anthology *Northern Numbers* (1920-2) until his death in 1978 MacDiarmid was without doubt the most artistically impressive Scotsman of his time. Novelists such as Compton Mackenzie and Neil Gunn and Fionn Mac Colla expressed some of his ideas in fictional form while Eric Linklater portrayed him as "Hugh Skene" in *Magnus Merriman* (1934); dramatists (for example Robert McLellan and Alexander Reid) mounted MacDiarmidian spectacles on the stage; poets shaped their lines in what they hoped were the cadences of the author of *A Drunk Man Looks at the Thistle*. There was unquestionably an aesthetic extrapolated from MacDiarmid's practice as a poet but there was nowhere available a meditative essay expounding his point of view in a way that would be helpful to writers, painters and musicians. Most of MacDiarmid's prose was produced under intolerable pressure to meet deadlines or fill an urgent propagandist need. Even *Lucky Poet* (1943), completed in the Shetland island of Whalsay in 1941, was written quickly and put together at a time when the Second World War looked as if it might indeed be the war to end all wars—the Last World War. *Aesthetics in Scotland* is an unusually contemplative piece for MacDiarmid and only occasionally exhibits the fierce polemical anger that characterises most of his published prose.

In expansive mood, MacDiarmid surveys the state of art in Scotland and makes a general case for more culture. Now that this essay has, posthumously, materialised in print it is possible to see exactly how MacDiarmid regarded the aesthetic implications of the artistic revolution he had unleashed on Scotland. MacDiarmid's central contention is that art needs aesthetics because it is only properly appreciated on an intellectual level.

Totally opposed to the notion that the artist should simplify his art in order to make it easily accessible to the public, MacDiarmid argues that it is the responsibility of "most people" (or "the feck" as he calls them in his poetry) to lift themselves up into the Olympian heights inhabited by the great artists. He observes that "[most people] do not—or will not—understand that they can only receive from works of art in proportion to what they bring to them". By defending modernists like Joyce and Picasso from the insults of the Philistines, he condemns the mental lethargy that substitutes platitudinous "commonsense" for a cerebral response to a work of art.

All through his long career MacDiarmid was attacked by those who disliked his élitist attitude to art and his high-and-mighty approach to politics. The man of the people who castigated "the feck" was also (at times) a Scottish Nationalist and a card-carrying Communist with an abiding interest in Social Credit. The result was not so much inconsistency as complexity arising from his vision of a world in which the new saviour of society is the artist who leads the people ever upwards into increasingly subtle aesthetic spheres. In *Aesthetics in Scotland* he combines his intellectual élitism with a belief in the untapped resources of the Scottish people. He categorises "the man-in-the-street and his wife" as culturally underprivileged and looks forward to the day when the spiritual light of the Scotttish Renaissance will dawn in Scotland so that all Scots will be in a position to comprehend their own culture:

> The mass of the people will react all right if they get a chance. It is the stupid conservatism of their self-styled "betters" that is the danger . . . Amateurism has always been the curse of the arts in modern Scotland—amateurism, and, along with it, the inveterate predilection to "domesticate the issue" . . . the progress of the Arts in Scotland is dependent upon . . . the wider appreciation and striving after the highest possible standard.

In developing his argument—which amounts to a cultural revolution and new educational programme for Scotland—MacDiarmid admits a new name to his pantheon. A. S. Dallas is added to the ranks of the great Scotsmen considered intellectually adventurous enough to be given MacDiarmid's blessing. Dallas, and other unorthodox authorities, are quoted (often at great length) as witnesses to MacDiarmid's vigorous prosecution of a society in which everyman will strive to be an intellectual superman. Given his faith in the necessity of extremes meeting in a provocative manner—of contradictions coalescing in a quintessentially Celtic synthesis—MacDiarmid emphasises the traditional values implicit in modernism (at least the modernism he has in mind):

> It is a very great mistake to allow an excessive contemporaneity to make us contemptuous of or indifferent to the very different standards of previous periods. There is also the fact—and this is especially true of a country like Scotland where the national

> tradition has been hopelessly fragmented or driven underground and very few people, if any, possess a complete knowledge of it, that the kind of reading I am recommending is likely to bring to light again all sorts of people of whom sight has been undeservedly lost and who ought to be kept in mind and esteemed at their true worth.

What the following pages clarify, then, is MacDiarmid's own aesthetic which is a very metaphysical matter—hence his critical comments on the Scottish commonsense school of philosophy. MacDiarmid wanted to undermine the traditional scepticism of the Scottish people and make them believe in the spiritual qualities he himself expressed as an artist. Though written in 1950 (with a coda from 1965) *Aesthetics in Scotland* has a timely appeal. It is MacDiarmid's most sustained essay on a subject that clearly fascinated him and contains a message of hope for the country he enriched by his example.

When, in 1965, MacDiarmid reread *Aesthetics in Scotland* he felt heartened enough to add that concluding paragraph recording some "signs of a genuine advance" in aesthetic awareness in Scotland. Since then the situation has improved considerably. MacDiarmid's death jolted the world into the realisation that a truly great one had gone and publishers were quick to commission books investigating the range and depth of his poetry. The worth of some of those in MacDiarmid's circle was likewise given some overdue attention. Francis George Scott, MacDiarmid's musical mentor, was the subject of a biography (by Maurice Lindsay) and celebrated on a centenary recording of his songs (by Isobel Buchanan and Malcolm Donnelly). In 1971 the Richard Demarco Gallery mounted an exhibition of the work of William McCance and there were several important exhibitions (in London's Hayward Gallery and elsewhere) of the art of William Johnstone whose autobiography *Points in Time* appeared in 1980.

Inevitably it was Scottish literature that attracted most comment in books as diverse as Francis Russell Hart's *The Scottish Novel* (1978), Trevor Royle's *Companion to Scottish Literature* (1983) and the present writer's *Modern Scottish Literature* (1983) which is dedicated to the memory of MacDiarmid. It was never MacDiarmid's intention to attract disciples but rather to generate a movement which would result in political independence and (consequently) aesthetic dignity for Scotland; he was fond of saying that to be international one had to have a nation to be "inter" about. This emphasis on political autonomy was a formulation of the individuality he valued so highly in his poetry. In *A Drunk Man Looks at the Thistle* MacDiarmid advised his countrymen:

> And let the lesson be—to be yersel's,
> Ye needna fash gin it's to be ocht else.
> To be yersel's—and to mak' that worth bein'.
> Nae harder job to mortals has been gi'en.

It is salutary to see how this impulse towards individuality has been taken up by post-MacDiarmidian Scottish artists in every field. The younger figurative painters of Scotland, such as John Bellany and Alexander Moffat, have used an expressive pictorial language that speaks for Scotland in an eloquent way and in doing so have allied a particular national outlook with a general continental consciousness. Bellany's use of Celtic imagery, for example, as well as his international reputation, recalls the precedent of Charles Rennie Mackintosh who was, in 1900, invited to contribute his decorative ideas to the Vienna of the Secession. In music Ronald Stevenson and Edward McGuire (both drawn to classical and traditional compositional forms) have extended the indigenous eclecticism of Francis George Scott. The Scottish theatre underwent something of a histrionic renaissance in the 1970s while the Scottish cinema of the 1980s could claim a talent as visually taut as that of Bill Forsyth.

None of the artists cited above is to be regarded only as a MacDiarmid disciple; yet none could have done so much without the example of MacDiarmid. In all his work MacDiarmid stressed the quality of Scotland as a nation that could build an artistically assertive future by recalling the giants of the past and putting the present under powerful aesthetic pressure. It is not enough, MacDiarmid suggested, to take Scotland for granted and allow the defeatist state of the nation to continue. It is necessary to give the Scottish tradition something of a traumatic shock to bring Scotland to life again:

> The thistle rises and forever will,
> Getherin' the generations under 't.
> This is the monument o' a' they were,
> And a' they hoped and wondered.

The wonder will never cease if MacDiarmid is, at last, to have his way.

ALAN BOLD
Balbirnie, September 1983

Note on the Text

Aesthetics in Scotland exists in two forms: there is a manuscript of the work in Edinburgh University Library and a typescript at the People's Palace Museum, Glasgow. The text of six missing manuscript pages is contained in the typescript.

Edinburgh University Library acquired the MS of *Aesthetics in Scotland* in 1967 as part of a collection gathered by Kulgin Duval and Colin Hamilton. From internal evidence the bulk of this manuscript can be dated 1950 on account of two specific references: MacDiarmid refers to the publication "the other day" of Eric Newton's *The Meaning of Beauty* (1950) and later comments on the Edinburgh Festival production of John Home's tragedy *Douglas* (1756) which was revived at the Festival in 1950 with Sybil Thorndike as Lady Randolph and her son-in-law Douglas Campbell as Young Norval. As the notes on p. 96 explain, the EUL MS has been augmented by two additional passages, one from 1952 and one from 1965.

The typescript in the People's Palace has clearly been prepared from the EUL MS as it is identical apart from the two additional passages noted on p. 96. This 1950 TS was discovered by Andrew Brown, the Administration Officer of Kelvingrove Art Gallery, in 1972 when he passed it to Michael Donnelly, organiser of "Hugh MacDiarmid: An Exhibition of Poetry and Propaganda" (People's Palace, 1972). The typescript is now kept in the People's Palace.

In conversation with the present writer Michael Donnelly, now Field Officer of the People's Palace, persuasively suggested that since the 1950 TS was found among papers at Kelvingrove Art Gallery it was probably sent to T. J. Honeyman, Director of Glasgow Art Galleries and Museums. In his autobiography *Art and Audacity* (1971) Honeyman states that he was one of twenty-two people who applied for the Director's job in 1939:

> C. M. Grieve (Hugh MacDiarmid) had a shot at [applying for the post]. We had been together on the staff of the 42nd General Hospital in Salonika in World War I. I often wondered how he would have tackled the job. Poetry in Scotland would have suffered, but as a dynamic personality he might have stirred things up. I remember on a special occasion attending a conference aimed at starting an Academy of Scottish Art and Letters. My contribution to the discussion was "What's the use of having Christopher Grieve in anything like this? He always resigns." "It's a lie," came back the defiance. "I get expelled."

Also quoted in the book is a comment MacDiarmid made when, after World War Two, Honeyman withdrew a letter of resignation he had sent to Glasgow Corporation:

> It gave Hugh MacDiarmid a chance to have a smack at Bridie and me. His comment was "The two most recent disasters to afflict Scotland have been the withdrawal of Honeyman's resignation and the return of James Bridie from America." (Bridie had set out for a spell of writing for films in Hollywood but returned after one week in new York.)

Honeyman is mentioned, albeit in passing, with honour in *Aesthetics in Scotland*.

While working on the forthcoming edition of *The Letters of Hugh MacDiarmid*, the present writer came across the following passage in a letter of 20 October 1950 to Francis George Scott:

> My essay on Aesthetics in Scotland—part of which I am to deliver in the Spring as a public (Glasgow Corporation) lecture—will be published in pamphlet form in April or May. I finished it a month or so ago.

This establishes that the original manuscript was completed in Dungavel House in (probably) September 1950. Honeyman doubtless found the work much too long to publish as a pamphlet and so the typescript remained among his official papers at Kelvingrove Art Gallery. Evidently, from the additions he made to the EUL MS MacDiarmid twice returned to the work with thoughts of publication. There the matter rested until now.

I am most grateful to Dr John Hall of Edinburgh University Library for letting me see the manuscript and providing me with a photocopy of the EUL MS; and to Michael Donnelly of the People's Palace for discussing the 1950 TS with me. I must also thank Mrs Valda Grieve and Michael Grieve for allowing me to edit the text.

A.B.

Aesthetics in Scotland

by Hugh MacDiarmid

IN a recent article Mr. John Tonge said: "That factory of the arts, the modern art school, could help by teaching the young artist not only his craft, but by clarifying the role of the 20th Century Scottish artist in Scotland and in society. The national tradition is some kind of a handrail in this 'museum without walls'."

The reference in the last sentence is to M. André Malraux's book, *Psychologie de l'Art*, published by Roto-Sadag in Geneva last year. Further reference will be made to it later. But the increasing sense and use of our national tradition in the way suggested by Mr. Tonge has been an outstanding feature of the past ten to twelve years and has borne good fruit.

Mr. Tonge himself was a pioneer in this connection with his admirable little book, *The Arts of Scotland*, published in 1938 at the time of the Burlington House Exhibition of Scottish Art. It will be remembered that Sir William Llewellyn, the then President of the Royal Academy, confessed that he had had no idea before he saw that Exhibition that Scotland had such a rich and distinctive tradition of its own in the art of painting, and a tradition so dissimilar to the English tradition. The Exhibition was, he declared, an eye-opener. Most of the art critics in our leading British newspapers and cultural periodicals wrote in the same strain. It did not occur to any of them, however, to examine more deeply this extraordinary situation in which of two countries linked together under a common Crown and Parliament for two and a half centuries one of them remained utterly ignorant of, and indifferent to, so important a part of the other's life as its paintings, nor did it stimulate them to enquire whether or not the English, while seeing to it that their language, history, literature and other arts, had a virtual monopoly in our Scottish schools and colleges (without any reciprocal attention to their Scottish counterparts in the English educational system) were equally ignorant of Scottish literature, Scottish music, and, for the matter of that, the whole range of Scottish national affairs. It will be clear that the exclamations of astonished—and, in some quarters, incredulous—discovery evoked in England and elsewhere by the Burlington House Exhibition disclosed a very serious state of affairs and threw a thoroughly disconcerting light on the general assumption that the Scots-English relationship was a satisfactory one. It is obviously inevitable that a Union under which the arts of one country are almost entirely unknown to the other, while the arts of the latter, entirely different in character and tendency to its own, are given an overinfluence in the former through the educational system and through the press, platform, and other media of publicity, to the virtual exclusion of any attention whatever to its native products must be equally unsatisfactory in political, commercial, social and all other connections. These implications—which are responsible for the increasing nationalist ferment in Scotland during the past quarter of a century—have proved highly unpalatable to most of the English writers and speakers who have got so far as to realise them at all. Most of them have reacted by a "conspiracy of silence". Others have gone out of their way to belittle Scottish culture in one way or another. The bad feeling that exists in many quarters cannot always be hidden or camouflaged, however. It manifests itself occasionally as in the review of Mr. Stanley Cursiter's book, *Scottish Art*, in *The Listener* of 7th April 1949, which said: "Scotland is a long way off, even by train; but distance is not the factor which produces a national school of painting, and demonstrations of such a school in the smaller dependent countries [note that phrase!] are tatty, and, to the outsider, unconvincing to the edge of pathos. Out comes the brush. A great many names and a great many inferior pictures are dusted out of the corners and tidied together with a few good pictures into a school which no one else in the world acknowledges. It is a compulsion, and Mr. Cursiter, having directed the National Gallery at Edinburgh, could not escape. Yet how much stronger our impression of Scottish painting, or painting by Scotsmen, would be if Mr. Cursiter could blow off all the dust! We ourselves have to blow it off. We have to clean off Allan Ramsay, and Geddes and Raeburn and Wilkie, as well as a few altogether unfamiliar artists, who need pushing into our more sceptical sight. Mr. Cursiter quotes Northcote on a likeness of Queen Charlotte which Ramsay painted 'a profile, and slightly done, but it was a paragon of elegance. She had a fan in her hand; Lord how she held that fan!' Excellent; but the scope of Ramsay's power is not always acknowledged. It hardly *excites* Mr. Cursiter. Yet Allan Ramsay may seem to an English-man, remembering the portrait of his wife and some others which Mr. Cursiter reproduces, more deliciously appetising than any painter who ever came down from the north. But is he Scottish, or is he European? Or even English? Mr. Cursiter might have told us more, for example, of Ramsay's assistant David Martin, and more of Thomas Graham (1840-1906), in deference to two of the pictures reproduced; he might have told us less of the many Victorian academicians and the late Victorian namby-pambyists of one type and another. But he is kindly. He is mild rather than critical or selective and he has to keep the Scottish flag well aloft. To those who might be Englishmen or Frenchmen or Americans matters up north seem to go like this: 'There were painters called Impressionists in France, whom the world thinks of very highly. You know in Scotland we had a painter called McTaggart who painted a little impressionistically. *We* had our Impressionist. What a great painter our Impressionist was!' . . . Whereas he was not. He painted pictures (out with the red jacket before the Lowland bull) which are frail, flat, and provincial. There it is . . . there indeed is the trouble of the dust-panning of a pseudo-national school: it must capture the eyes of the Scottish young and the Scottish innocent. Provinciality must be posed as the real thing in the guise of patriotism. It would be better patriotism to act less patriotically."

The Listener is one of the official organs of a public Corporation. The vicious anti-Scottish attitude of that anonymous spokesman of the English *herren-volk* must therefore be taken as a reflection of Government policy, and as an accurate index of the general attitude of the English *cognoscenti* to Scottish cultural issues. Nor is it an isolated phenomenon. *The Listener* is closed to Scottish talks—only the talks from the English programmes are reproduced in it. That is characteristic.

It is not a matter only of today, however. Fears are expressed in many quarters lest the Scottish discontent with Londonisation should lead to anti-English feeling in Scotland. Right down our history, however, anti-Scottish feeling has been strong in England. Scotland has produced no anti-English writers to compare with the whole sequence of anti-Scottish writers from Charles Churchill and Dr. Johnson to our own day who have been so marked an element in English literary history.

That this deplorable state of affairs does not apply to painting only, but to the whole range of Scottish arts and affairs, is clear from any consideration of the history of the independent Scottish literary tradition. I can only give one illustration here. In his splendid study of the 15th Century Scottish poet, Robert Henryson, Professor Marshall W. Stearns of Cornell University says: "The reputation of Robert Henryson is still in the process of being established. Even his own countrymen found little merit in him until comparatively recently. The first adequate estimate of the poet was made by William Ernest Henley in 1880. . . . Recognition of Henryson in the United States was even more delayed. In 1888 James Russell Lowell condemned fifteenth-century Scottish poetry in general and the Middle Scots dialect in particular, while four years later Professor T. R. Lounsbury observed [in the very tone of *The Listener* review I have just quoted] that Henryson 'is one of those early writers whom Scottish patriotism struggles energetically to consider a poet'." The tide began to turn in England after that, however. W. W. Skeat in 1897 singled out Henryson's *Testament of Cresseid* as the best Chaucerian poem, and in the following year Professor George Saintsbury said of Henryson's poems: "The total bulk is not large, but the merit is, for the 15th Century more particularly, very high, and the variety of directions in which it is shown is extremely remarkable", and he ranked the *Testament of Cresseid* with, if not above, the best work of the century. If space permitted, I could show that in many other directions Scottish work is still grossly underprized or completely neglected, and the extremely belated rehabilitation of Henryson in his proper place as a great poet after the lapse of several centuries is only a pointer to the sort of revaluation or rescue work which must yet be effected in many fields of Scottish Arts and Letters.

Far more serious, however, is the indisputable fact that the Scottish people themselves were—and the vast majority of them still are—as ignorant as the English with regard to the Scottish tradition in literature and the arts, and, indeed, with regard to Scottish interests in the whole range of affairs. It is that ignorance and indifference that has at long last begun to be rectified in some measure. But only the fringe of it has been touched so far. Far too many Scots are still utterly insensitive to the arts—a higher proportion, I think, than can be found in any other Western European country. One of Scotland's greatest men, David Hume, the philosopher, blandly admitted that he was constitutionally incapable of taking any interest in any of the arts. The Scottish novelist, Tobias Smollett, was equally uninterested. I am afraid that what Mr. William Power says in his book, *Literature And Oatmeal*, is still only too true of a very large section of our people.

"In a compartment of the Flying Scotsman, roaring north along the central rock-ridge of the Merse," says Mr. Power, "I began to dilate to a companion on the part that the canyon of Pease Dean, near Cockburnspath, had played in Scots history. I spoke of Cromwell and the Battle of Dunbar, Scott, and *The Bride of Lammermoor*. A man in a landward corner of the compartment broke in: 'Ugh! That's history. An' literature, I suppose'. He was burly and fiftyish, with a bristly moustache. He wore a good suit of rough brown tweed, and there was a horseshoe pin in his ugly tie. His boots had cost a good deal more than sixty shillings. I guessed him to be a prosperous contractor and general merchant in a country town, grazing beasts on a couple of 'led' farms.

'Don't the history and literature of your own country mean anything to you?' I asked.

'Not a bit. Just nonsense. The stuff we used to get in school. Ugh! . . . ' His contempt was beyond articulate expression. In the attitude of this man, I reflected, there was more than mere indifference. There was a positive element. History and literature, particularly those of Scotland, were somehow inimical to his way of life. He had a bad conscience concerning them. The outlook in such matters that usually confronts one in England is curiously different. It is one of amiable nescience. Anyone who begins to talk of history or literature in a chance company is listened to with polite inattention, as if he were a foreigner who was inadvertently speaking his own language. But nobody is ever rude about it."

To blame all this on Calvinism in Scotland is stupid. It not only ignores the facts which are admirably set out in Dr. Mary Ramsay's *Calvin And Art*. It ignores also the fact that it is quite unjust to attribute to Calvinism a crude Philistinism which was, in fact, bred by the Industrial Revolution and aggravated by the loss of our own national roots. It ignores also the fact that on the admission of the Church of Scotland a third of our entire population today have no church connection of any kind, while another large section are Roman Catholics and have no more aesthetic interest or sensitivity than either the heirs of the Calvinists or the neo-Pagans. Then, again, what are we to make of the fact that Calvinism in other countries—Holland, for example—did not prevent great schools of painting? While efforts have been made in the last quarter of a century to correct this deplorable anti-aestheticism of the Scottish people, these efforts have so far been of a very sporadic and superficial kind, and have not yet succeeded in ramming home even to the most alert of our countrymen the great fact stated by the German poet, Hölderlin, that "Nothing is so difficult to learn as the mastery over our natural national gifts."

Hölderlin put the matter very clearly—and what he says in the following passage must be applied to our own case and thoroughly learned and digested before there can be a real national awakening in regard to the arts in Scotland—when he wrote: "It sounds paradoxical, but I repeat and leave it to you to test in theory and practice, natural qualities always become in the process of learning the lesser merit. On that account the Greeks are less masters of sacred passion because it was innate in them; on the other hand they are excellent at representing from Homer onwards, because this extraordinary man was large-minded enough to appropriate and make use of Western Junonian clear-headedness for his Apolline sphere, and thus truly to assimilate elements foreign to him. With the Germans the opposite was the case, and it was for that very reason necessary for them to study the Greeks, both their nature and their art, in order to gain knowledge of themselves and what should be the aim of their art. But we have to win knowledge of our own faculties just as much as of those of others. That is why the Greeks are indispensable to us. Only we shall not be able to equal them in the qualities natural to us, because, as was said already, mastery over one's own nature is the most difficult of all."

One of the most characteristic American cartoons I have seen depicted a prosperous citizen being sucked down a manhole in Fifth Avenue by an octopus. A listless crowd stands round and watches his agonised face on the point of disappearing. A prosperous citizen in a top-hat remarks to his friend: "Anything will collect a crowd in New York."

Thanks to the activities of Dr. Honeyman and the Saltire Society, the Arts Council, and other bodies, Art is beginning to attract increasing crowds in Scotland today. Before going on to ask what art, and to what effect, I must make it clear that I do not think Art in Scotland is in the grip of an octopus and being sucked down a drain. On the contrary I do not think the public response to art in Scotland was ever greater in quantity or better in quality than it is today or the prospects better not only for art in Scotland and a genuine appreciation of it among our people, but also—a far harder thing—for the consolidation and development of our distinctive Scottish tradition, and for constructive criticism (that is to say, criticism helpful to the artists) and the elucidation and elaboration of a complementary aesthetics and the building-up of an adequately impressive organisation to secure for Scottish art a fair share of recognition and attention throughout the world. In short, we are, in my opinion, getting past the stage now in which there seemed a real danger of our becoming bogged not long ago—the stage of having "all the culture of the world on tap and none of our own". It has been said, "If we want an art that will express the values of our democratic society, we must provide the artist with a growing audience whose judgment he does not despise". I think we are building up in Scotland today an adequate public of that sort, despite the fact that art education in the ordinary schools is poor, because most teachers are not expected to have any standards of appreciation or knowledge beyond those of the general public, and specialised art teaching is bad, because it has to turn out designers who are neither required nor encouraged to do good work—although there has perhaps been a little improvement in that connection in the past year or two. But so far as the public at large is concerned, any art teaching they may have had is vastly supplemented by the tremendous number of excellent art-books of all kinds available to them at little cost or through the public library system; and by admirable radio talks; and by the fact that art treasures of all kinds are open to their inspection to an infinitely greater extent than has been the case at any previous period in human history.

Mr. Tonge's book to which I have referred is not only an admirable introduction to the subject, giving all the most essential factual information in a lucid and highly readable form, but it was the first book on its subject which was highly intelligent, widely informed, thoroughly up-to-date, and, in short, deserving of shelf-room alongside the average of the books of real value produced in the past half-century or so on the arts of other small European countries. Most of these countries, however, have scores of such books to their credit. This was literally Scotland's first. There had been other books on the subject, but they were all hopelessly out-of-date and in any case were little more than unintelligent catalogues of names, diversified with insignificant personalia, chit-chat, comments of the most hackneyed kind, stock platitudes, banal bromides and clap-trap generally.

As Mr. Tonge himself said in his preface: "There is no book giving the kind of all-round view of art and *Kunstgewerbe* popularised on the Continent in such works as Hamann's *Geschichte der Kunst* or Burckhardt's *Renaissance*"; and he goes on to say that while the two volumes published by Messrs. Maclehose after the 1888 and 1901 Exhibitions respectively—namely *Scottish National Memorials* and *Scottish History And Life*—bring together a good deal of expert information, the pages he had devoted to the crafts of Scotland had had to be supplemented by reference to Mr. J. Arnold Fleming's writings on pottery and glass, the literature on Communion Plate, and other specialised works.

The rapidly developing momentum of our contemporary Scottish Movement is shown by the fact that the few years which have elapsed since the publication of Mr. Tonge's book have been signalised by a whole succession of books and pamphlets far superior in every way to anything previously available. We are entitled to assume that that indicates a corresponding growth of a well-informed and intensely interested public in our midst. The publications I have in mind include Mr. Ian Finlay's *Scotland*, his *Art in Scotland* and his *Scottish Crafts*, Mr. Stanley Cursiter's *Scottish Art*, Dr. Honeyman's monograph on Leslie Hunter, and the two volumes now published in Messrs. Wm. MacLellan's Modern Scottish Painters series, namely *The New Scottish Group* and *Scottish*

Painters: *Donald Bain*. To these must be added the excellent 'Scottish Tradition' pamphlets published by the Saltire Society, and including *Pottery* by Iain Paul, *Burgh Architecture* by Iain Lindsay, *Silver* by Ian Finlay, *Printed Books* by W. R. Beattie, and *Photography* by R. O. Dougan. Mention must also be made of *The Scottish Art Review*, the quarterly magazine of the Glasgow Art Gallery and Museums Association, which has now developed into more than a Glasgow publication of restricted interest, and is reaching out into the wider field of art appreciation in general. All these together with the lectures given under the auspices of the Saltire Society, some of the talks on the Scottish BBC, and various other activities in Scotland today, amount to nothing less than a revolution compared with the position twenty-five years ago.

This development has been given the general name of the Scottish Renaissance Movement—a name which does not imply that that has been achieved, but simply that it is what is being aimed at. It has been remarked that interest in the corresponding arts of other countries is never keener than where a revival movement is afoot in a nation's own arts. Scotland has an unparalleled record of international interest and interaction, and it is good to see this feature so prominent again in the art products, writings and speeches of those who are most active in the Scottish Movement today. Not only has the level of debate risen immensely—not only is a far higher degree of intelligence and wealth of information and the power to assimilate and apply it being manifested, but in books like Mr. Tonge's and Mr. Finlay's at any rate real and very able attempts are made to grapple with the basic psychological and philosophical problems and to deduce the significance of these in relation to the ecology and ethos of our people. We find Mr. Tonge, for example, dealing with M. Henri Focillon's terms, *espace-milieu* as opposed to *espace limite*—that is to say, constructed with reference to space and not framed off from it like the Pyramids or the Parthenon, and going on to say: "The filigree technique so common in Celtic art presents a very obvious example of an art in which it is difficult to say whether the tangible forms or the immaterial intervals are the more important."

Again he says: "The New Town that Edinburgh built when, after centuries of turmoil, she turned her back on Prince Charles and Celtic Scotland, is so different from that of the Old Town of Edinburgh as to raise the question of whether such a classicism is in Scotland part of the artistic cycle into which Adama van Scheltema resolves all artistic movements, or a departure from a racial norm, or both. For Celtic Art comes within Worringer's category of Nordic Arts, and from his viewpoint Scotland, in the neo-Greek movement, could be regarded as indulging in something like the German *Sachlichkeit*, a merely temporary reaction from the characteristic Nordic *Expressionismus*."

Mr. Tonge sums up his whole position in the following passage, I think. "Scottish art as a whole—one must not forget the smooth facades and ordered simplicity of the New Town of Edinburgh—is much more involved and restless and dynamic than English art, and these characteristics we find in the asymmetrical intricate organic Celtic art. Scottish architecture—and architecture is the mother of the arts in Scotland no less than elsewhere—at its most characteristic evolves like a cellular structure, not from the tectonic piecing together of elements in classical fashion. It should not be forgotten, too, when the filigree technique of Celtic brooches, or the patterning of the Crosses is under consideration, that precisely the same technique characterises the consummate and intricate atonal art-music of the composers of piobroch, some of the greatest of whose works date from as recently as the 17th Century."

Writing of Rosslyn Chapel, Mr. Tonge says that its "rich ornament people who think of Scotland only as chaste and severe have been tempted to attribute to Burgos or Oviedo—to anyone except the Gael. Foreign workmen helped to build the chapel, as they did Holyrood, and there was foreign influence too; but when was there not foreign influence in the Middle Ages? There is nothing exotic in the plan, and the ornament is Celtic—not archaistic, but adapting intertwining coils and the rest to mediaeval ends. Its ornate qualities derive not from contemporary Renaissance work, which was relatively simple, but from the Celtic love of elaboration. The makers of Rosslyn did with English Gothic what the Makars did with the English tongue. Precisely the same juxtaposition of incongruous motives, the same crowded and firmly controlled ornament, is found in William Dunbar's aureate diction. And like Dunbar—Rosslyn is either warmly admired or as heartily hated."

Mr. Ian Finlay is in general agreement with Mr. Tonge in his insistence on the supreme importance of our Gaelic background. That point of view is so generally accepted by the leading controversialists on the subject of the arts in Scotland today (I share it fully myself) that it is desirable perhaps to quote a critic who is not a Scotsman on the subject. This is what Dr. Herbert Read says in his book, *The Meaning of Art*, and, before quoting it, I may refer gratefully to the period in the 20s during which Dr. Read occupied the Chair of Fine Arts in Edinburgh University and stirred up the dovecots there with his lively modernistic doctrines and impatience with pompous humbugs.

"The ornament of the early Celtic period," says Dr. Read, "is linear, geometric and abstract; the type most familiar is the interlaced ribbon or plaited ornament vulgarised in present-day 'Celtic' tombstones. It is seen in all its purity in the Book of Kells, the eighth-century manuscript belonging to Trinity College, Dublin. The real nature of this ornament has been well described by a German historian of art, Lamprecht, in the following words: 'There are certain simple motives whose interweaving and commingling determine the character of this ornament. At first there is only the dot, the line, the ribbon; later the curve, the circle, the spiral, the zig-zag, and an S-shaped decoration are employed. Truly no great wealth of motives! But what variety is attained by the manner of their employment! Here they run parallel, then entwined, now latticed, now knotted, now plaited, then again brought through one another in a symmetrical checker of knotting and plaiting. Fantastically confused patterns are thus evolved, whose puzzle asks to be unravelled, whose convolutions seem alternately to seek and avoid each other, whose component parts, endowed as it were with sensibility, captivate sight and sense in passionately vital movement."

Dr. Read goes on to say that this non-organic, super-organic type of art is "a mode of expression in direct contrast to the classical mode, which is organic, naturalistic, serene and satisfying. The significance of the Northern mode lies precisely in its life-denying qualities, its completely abstract character;

and in this character, in these qualities, one must see a reflection of the spiritual life of these Northern people—'the heavily oppressed inner life of Northern humanity', as Worringer has called it. Into this gloomy and abstract field of art, the symbols of Christianity come like visitants from an exotic land. In a prickly nest of geometrical lines, two birds of paradise will settle, carrying in their beaks a bunch of Eastern grapes. David comes with his harp and the three children in the furnace; Adam and Eve, and the sacrifice of Isaac, are represented in panels reserved among the bands of abstract ornament; and finally the stone is dominated by Christ in Glory and the company of angels. Such stones still stand where they were erected centuries ago in Ireland and Scotland; and no monuments in the world are so moving in their implications; they symbolise ten thousand years of human history, and represent that history at its spiritual extremes, nearest and farthest from the mercy of God."

From some of the phrases in that paragraph I think Dr. Read has mistaken the matter. Worringer was referring to the Scandinavian peoples who are extremely neurotic and heavily-oppressed in their inner life. Such terms are quite inapplicable to the Gael. The Gaelic people were gay and fantastic. Classical Gaelic literature is merry and quite unburdened by the spiritual excesses subsequently wished on the Gaelic genius during the so-called "Celtic Twilight" period. Not twilight but the clear sun was the symbol of the classical Gaelic spirit. But Gaeldom stands outside Europe altogether. Its affiliations are with the East. And it is not to Worringer's Nordic Arts but to the arts of the East we must look when we seek to understand Gaelic Art.

In one of my own books,[1] have said with reference to

this matter, "The ideas of the East-West synthesis and the Caledonian antisysygy merge into one and lie at the root of any understanding of, for example, that great Scottish musical achievement, the *piobaireachd* or great pipe music, and it is impossible to communicate any idea of pibroch to people who are not effectively seized of this joint-idea. Mr. Harold Picton's *Early German Art and Its Origins, from the beginning to about 1050* (published in 1939) emerges from a grasp of related factors in the same field. This important book is the first in English—and probably in any language—to give a general account of what may be termed the non-classical standpoint of the origins of German art and thus of Northern European art generally. In an appreciative foreword Professor Josef Strzygowski, the leading authority on early European art, confirms the validity of the orientation adopted by Mr. Picton in this work. Tracing the characteristics of Germanic art from the earliest beginnings, the author makes clear the large part played by Syria, Armenia, and the East in general in the development of the arts of Building, Ornament, Painting, Carving, Goldsmith's Work, Enamel and Sculpture. He shows how the influence of the South often perverted into naturalism the talent of the Germans for pattern, fantasy, and abstraction, while the effect of the East often confirmed and stimulated that talent. One of the most important features of the book is the wealth of well-reproduced illustrations with which the wave of Eastern influence, and the backwash of this influence from Ireland, is brought out."

I have quoted Mr. Tonge's references to pibroch music and to Dunbar's poetry in connection with the arts of painting and sculpture—and I might have culled similar analogies drawn from a wide intimacy with science, literature and history from the pages of Mr. Ian Finlay and others—for the special reason that they illustrate a pronounced and I think very valuable tendency which has developed to an enormous extent in certain countries and has only shown the most tentative beginnings so far in Scotland where it can certainly be pursued immensely further with vast profit. It has been remarked that, like all other sciences, that of aesthetics has undergone decisive changes during the past three-quarters of a century, both in method and in scope. "It is," says one writer, "difficult even to compare the present with the early stage in which it is still to be found in some countries, where the science has remained under the spell of narrow preoccupations with theories of beauty and with those based on idealistic metaphysics. The term aesthetics as it has been used during the last century is derived from Baumgarten's work, *Aestetica* (published in 1750), but a strictly scientific view of aesthetics was first developed by Kant in his *Kritik der Urteilskraft*, published in 1790. Recent decades have shown an intensification of aesthetic activities such as has never been known before. Art history has been developed from a descriptive and classifying doctrine to a science which takes into account not only the stylistic aspects but also deeper connections with the general ideas of mankind. The Swiss, Heinrich Wöllflin, is the chief exponent of the first line of thought (*Die Grundbegriffe der Kunstgeschichte*), and the Viennese, Max Dvorak, who saw the history of art as a history of the human spirit, expounds it in his *Kunstgeschichte als Geistesgeschichte*. Dvorak liberated art history from the methods applied by the natural sciences. Modern psychology has had a tremendous impact on art history and art theory; a new term had to be invented to cover the entire field of knowledge. This German term, *Kunstwissenschaft*, the science of art, includes not only the history of art but also art theory and art criticism, the development and periodicity of styles and techniques, the relation of spiritual culture and material civilisation (as in Jacob Burckhardt and certain Marxist thinkers), and the analysis of the creative processes themselves (as in Freud, Jung, Lévy-Brühl, Worringer), from which point of view the life of the artist, his journals, his manifestoes and theories became of greater importance. The interrelations of the arts—as the different forms of expression of the human psyche and probably the purest sources of human experience, and the crisis of art as a symptom of the spiritual crisis of our highly-mechanised life—are the latest fields of research. With this widening of interest in the arts, the literature of the subject has become more diverse. The mass of popular books on art is overwhelming. Their characteristic is a kind of general or panoramic approach to the problems and "isms" of art and its personalities, based mainly upon illustrations, often uncritical and subjective. General histories of art and critical biographies, when written by experts, represent the next step. A wide range of psychological, philosophical, and sociological works are also devoted today to problems of aesthetics; they are written by scientists who, like the late Dr. A. N. Whitehead, are convinced that "the most fruitful, because the most neglected, starting-point of philosophic thought is that section of value theory which we term aesthetic".

A model book in this connection is Professor Charles Gauss's *The Aesthetic Theories of French Artists*, published early this year. In it, Professor Gauss takes the writings of modern artists as the basis of research. Beginning with Courbet and his manifestoes on realism, the book goes on to the theories of impressionism of the two great independents, Cézanne and Renoir, of Symbolism (Synthetism) and Fauvism (Gauguin, Denis, Matisse), of early Cubism (Gleizes, Metzinger), and finally of Surrealism (Breton, Ernst, Dali). Professor Gauss challenges the views of such theorists as Curt Ducasse who insisted that it was wrong to see in the artist an expert, because the production of works of art was something very different from dealing with theoretical questions. Professor Gauss shows clearly how these manifestoes can be critically used to elucidate the new methods and the revolutionary character of contemporary art. The book has a second outstanding merit—and this seems to have been the author's main concern—and that is to show that each aesthetic theory reflects a philosophical background and that therefore the problems of the artist are the problems of the philosopher, namely the enigmas of the external world. It is revealing to see how realism and Comte's positivism as well as Saint Simon's social ideas are related; how impressionist theories of light coincide with the research work of Augustin Fresnel, Helmholz, and M. Chevreul; how the philosophical parallel of Renoir's repudiation of any connection between science and art is the Bergsonian metaphysic; and how there is an analogy between Cézanne's idea that artistic creation depends upon the acceptance of an ordering principle of sensation, and Poincaré's demonstration of the reason for hypotheses in scientific method. The inner connection of Symbolism and Fauvism with Schelling's romantic philosophy and with the anti-intellectualism in contemporary French thinking, is shown to be as convincing as the identity of the cubist theories, and the critique of scientific methodology made by Meyerson. The theoretical background of Surrealism, besides the Freudian and Jungian psychology, is also Hegel's principle of dialectic and Lobatschewsky's discovery of a non-Euclidean geometry. Such books as Professor Gauss's are important because they break down the barriers which specialisation has built up between the sciences. Specialisation prevents us achieving a unified picture of the world as reflected in all intellectual activities. It is the unification, the wholeness of an outlook on life, that is the sign of the maturity of a genuine culture.

We are a long way from anything of that sort in Scotland yet. Nevertheless progress is being made. As with Mr. Tonge's, the great virtue of Mr. Finlay's work is that it is the record of a mind earnestly striving to get away from vague abstractions, meaningless catchwords, and facile clichés. Both write with that vividness and conviction which come from living contact with the subject under discussion. This is something quite new in Scottish art-writing. And with that remark I come to the heart of my subject—"Aesthetics in Scotland". One of the few books of any consequence published in recent years dealing with the aesthetic doctrines of Scottish philosophers is a two-volume study in Italian by an Italian scholar, well-known to many of us in Scotland today, Signor Mario Rossi. His book is entitled *L'Estetica dell' Empirismo Inglese*, that is to say, *The Aesthetics of the English Empiricists*, and appeared in 1946 in a series published by the firm of Sansoni under the general title "Scrittori d'Estetica". I will not pause at the moment to object to the adjective English in the title, when half the Empiricist philosophers dealt with are in fact Scotsmen, including David Hume, Lord Kames, Dugald Stewart and others. Signor Rossi has no difficulty in showing, in his introduction, that the aesthetic theory of the Empiricists, so far as it could be called a theory, failed to establish "The true character of the universality of the beautiful", and that their illegitimate progress from the perceptions of the senses to the apprehension of universals vitiated the whole of their arguments, even those of Lord Shaftesbury which were directed to establishing the universality of the beautiful. Seen in the light of the progress in transcendental philosophy since Kant and of the more modern discoveries in the field of psychology, the common-sense aesthetics of the seventeenth and eighteenth centuries appear rather faded and only distinguished by the grace and urbanity of their presentation. They were not concerned with art in the sense in which we conceive the subject today at all. What they were concerned with was moral philosophy. None of them seem to have had any actual acquaintance with the arts or with artists and where they deal with the subject of beauty they do so in forms of more or less thinly disguised theology. None of them condescend to show any knowledge of or interest in objects of art. Blake stressed the importance of minute particulars and stigmatised those who traffic only in generalities as knaves and fools. And certainly the Scottish philosophers I have in mind avoided particulars like the plague. They wrote in fact *in vacuo* and that—and the nature of the presuppositions with which they came to their task—vitiated their work and makes it today, if not altogether unreadable, extremely transpontine and practically valueless. They knew and cared little or nothing about the arts—only about Art with a capital A, which means nothing at all.

The trouble with all these philosophers—Sir William Ferguson, Dr. Blair, Lord Kames, Adam Ferguson, Francis Hutcheson, and so on—and the trouble indeed with most of the Scots who have written on art until quite recently is, in fact, the trouble that afflicted the greatest writer on art Scotland has yet produced. I refer to John Ruskin. We are still apt to forget that Ruskin was a Scotsman. The trouble with Ruskin is described by R. H. Wilenski as follows: "He was addicted from childhood onwards to a drug which he was forced to take in daily doses in the nursery until he acquired the taste for it. In youth and maturity he fought against the abuse of the drug; but he fought in vain; when at last he was immuned by satiety his power of action was all spent. The drug, of course, was the emotive language of the Bible. Ruskin, as everyone knows, was made to read the Bible *aloud* every day in childhood and early youth. He was started at the beginning, taken through to the end, and then back to begin again. He was also made to memorise long sections of the text. This continued until he went to Oxford. He then knew by heart Exodus, Chapters XV and XX; Deuteronomy, Chapters XXXII; 2 Samuel, Chapter I from 17th verse to the end; 1st Kings, Chapter VIII; Psalms XXIII, XXXII, XC, XCI, CIII, CXIX, CXXXIX; Isaiah, Chapter LCIII; Matthew, Chapters V, VI, VII, Acts, Chapter XXVI; 1st Corinthians, Chapters XIII, XV; James, Chapter IV, and he had thousands of other phrases in his head. He continued to read the Bible as long as he read anything. He was always obsessed with the emotive rhythm, the sonority, the obscurity, the archaism, and awful associations of this living text within his brain. We shall never know to what extent the obsession impeded his power of thinking, but no one who has really studied his writing will, I am convinced, deny that this obsession fatally impeded the precise externalization of his thought. The remembered language continually intervened between the thought and its expression, and often sidetracked the thought itself. Ruskin, it is quite clear, struggled to use language as a means of precise communication. He fussed about the derivations of words to persuade himself that he was learning to use words with scientific care. But in fact he continually failed to achieve sustained control of his vocabulary. Again and again he began by making sentences in which the words exactly represent the thought; and then some remembered emotive words and phrases would rise to his mind's surface, and he would take first one sip of the fatal drug, and then another, till, finally, he would abandon the hard task of precise externalization of thought, and yield to the pleasure of making 'some sort of melodious noise about it'. Again and again a paragraph begins as precise writing, and ends as emotive rhetoric recalling the Bible. In book after book the words on the first few pages have no power themselves, but submissively obey the thought; then gradually the words become more Biblical, and so emotive, till, in the end, the thought is dancing to their tune."

There is a great deal more to be said about Ruskin than that, however. He was a man of indubitable genius. After a long period of obloquy and belittlement, he is now happily being restored in critical esteem. There have been many good books about him recently. But all that Mr. Wilenski says in the passage I have quoted is true enough; and the same thing is true of most of our Scottish philosophers. The same thing is still true of almost all of us, although few of us nowadays perhaps are over-dosed with the Bible. Yet thinking as distinct from rationalisation is extremely rare among us in every connection. There is even a widespread prejudice against the use of exact terminology. The general preference is for the time-honoured commonplaces, windy abstractions, and bromides. Careful study, thorough knowledge, and precise expression are generally at a discount. With all the facilities at their disposal nowadays most people steer clear of equipping themselves with information about the things they go to see. They do not—or will not—understand that they can only receive from works of art in proportion to what they bring to them. They continue to refuse to prepare themselves in any way, and, confronted with works of art, give vent to expressions of opinion of the most irresponsible and imbecilic kind—at the same time not hesitating to insist that every man is entitled to his own opinion and that their opinions are just as much entitled to consideration as anybody else's. It never occurs to them that they lack even the minimum basis for the formation of any opinion, and when they say, "Of course, I am not an expert", or "There's nothing highbrow about me", what they are really doing in regard to Art is what most of them also do in regard to Philosophy, or, as Thomas Davidson put it, "What shall we say of people who devote their time to reading novels written by miserable ignorant scribblers—many of them young, uneducated, and inexperienced—and who have hardly read a line of Homer or Sophocles or Dante or Shakespeare or Goethe, or even of Wordsworth or Tennyson, who would laugh at the notion of reading and studying Plato or Aristotle or Thomas Aquinas or Bruno or Kant or Rosmini? Are they not worse than the merest idiots, feeding prodigally upon swinish garbage, when they might be in their father's house, enjoying their portion of humanity's spiritual birthright? I know of few things more utterly sickening and contemptible than the self-satisfied smile of Philistine superiority with which many persons tell me, 'I am not a philosopher'. It simply means this, 'I am a stupid, low, grovelling fool, and I am proud of it'."

The type of all these Scottish philosophers—and indeed of the whole tribe of the pompous platitudinarians still so rife in Scottish public life—was Professor John Wilson, better known as "Christopher North", who occupied the chair of Moral Philosophy in Edinburgh University and knew so little about his subject that he was only able to keep going year after year in hand-and-mouth fashion, dependent on receiving in time for his next lecture a few notes and suggestions from a humble and little-known friend who supplied him in this way during the whole tenure of his Chair. "Wilson," says Miss Swann, his biographer, "never fully formulated his moral philosophy, for the Professor's ideas were always a little vague, and somewhat cloudy through lack of disciplined thought. His own doctrines were never quite fixed, and he stated publicly to the class at the close of his last session that he had all along been conscious there was some gap in it. He read widely, but in a haphazard and desultory way that never digested the reading so that it became an organic whole in his being; consequently he could not only contribute nothing new to philosophy but because he would not make the intellectual effort of absorbing his material had much ado to keep going as a lecturer. He shuffled along in a hand-to-mouth existence, fed with assiduous small scraps from Blair [the correspondent I referred to], in letters that arrived frequently. With a few crude notes of his own on the backs of envelopes, and chiefly with his gift of impassioned rhetoric, Wilson contrived to fill out the daily lecture and enflesh the few philosophical bones at his disposal with the juicy meat of his eloquence. The hungry sheep looked up and they were duly fed; but the more intelligent discovered later that there was surprisingly little sustenance in the fare provided by the persuasive shepherd. He was a hollow man, and he knew it better than anyone else. The knowledge made him awkward and *gauche* with Thomas Carlyle, because he sensed that Carlyle had looked within and seen his hollowness, as, of course, Carlyle had, with a most rare perception. Wilson, however, felt safe before the rest of the world, who accepted him at his face-value—provided that Blair stood behind him, and plied him with the means to keep up appearances."

While few of our people today have any exact knowledge of Scottish Philosophy—or the Common Sense Philosophy as it was called—and the names of Thomas Reid, Dugald Stewart, Sir William Hamilton, Francis Hutcheson and the others are hardly known at all save to students of the subject—a hangover from it conditions the general mentality of our people to an enormous extent. Speaking in Edinburgh University recently the Earl of Lindsay (Crawford) renounced Picasso's work and influence as destructive of all sound and normal values, all the decencies so laboriously built up in the course of civilisation. This sense of what is "sound and normal" is simply a hangover from Reid and the others. Is there any good basis for it? A great American scientist, Dr. Trigant Burrow, has recently written about it in the following terms: "Let us look into this attitude of normality, so called, upon which individuals and communities commonly pride themselves. Let us examine this social state of mind with its underlying trend toward conflict and antagonism.

We might consider the generally accepted covenants upon which this social fabric rests. For the prevailing pattern of 'normality' is as yet an unexplored field. It embodies habits of behaviour that we sacrosanct. Indeed, nothing so commands the fealty of human communities as the socially established average of conduct known by universal assent as normality. Nothing exerts a more irresistible influence over the processes of men than this criterion of behaviour embodied in the currently accepted social reaction-average, and this criterion of conduct dominates man's thinking and feeling today no less than in the earliest period of human history. The traditions of normality are preserved in literature, art, religion and philosophy.

"Its tenets are securely embalmed within the structure of the law. It is the warp and woof of politics, the raison d'être of physchiatry, the foundation of our educational systems. It enjoys the solemn endorsement of Church and State. Among all individuals, professional as well as lay, among all groups and all communities, it is 'normality' that regulates and determines the behaviour of family, home and country. It is the standard by which we measure all behaviour and indict as subversive or pathological whatever conduct deviates from this popularity cherished 'norm'. Very early in our analysis of groups we found that this social confederacy, this mentally conditioned state we credit as 'normality' possesses certain special and distinctive marks—marks that cannot be too strongly emphasised. In the first place, the standards of normality are completely arbitrary and mutable; they are alterable in accordance with personal volition. Though socially ubiquitous, this mental habitude rests upon no determinate premise; its dicta are wholly esoteric; it possesses no objectively stable constant. Besides, the motivation underlying this esoteric normality was found to activate equally the behaviour of the isolated neurotic and that of the socially adapted individual. It activates the teacher as well as the pupil, the governing alike with the governed, the parent no less than the child, the presumably strong and upstanding personality along with those presumed to be weak and ineffectual. As a gauge of interindividual conduct, 'normality' bears no dependable relation to reality, but is supported only by capricious community preconceptions. It is supported by one-sided ideologies, or, if I may recall the term I first used years ago, by arbitrary *social images*. What is more, normality as now constituted is sustained by a secret and unconscious prerogative that jealously preserves its partisan viewpoint against all inquiry. The shrine of normality at which all of us devoutly worship must on no account be examined into. The old-time religion is good enough for normality, and any investigation into its sacred rites and ordinances is taboo. For in its widebound conditioning, normality is always 'right' and the least infringement upon this interrelational mode of feeling and thinking calls forth a reflex defence reaction in individual and community.

"To question the prerogatives of this social consensus of behaviour is the unpardonable sin, the irreconcilable affront. By the universal manifestoes of unwritten law this criticism of human adaptation we call 'normality' is the great Sir Oracle. As the sworn custodian of the bidden ulterior aim, normality promptly frowns upon any suggestion that presumes to question its established dogmas. According to the adherents of normality, its subjective conviction of rightness and security leaves nothing to be desired. Enjoying supreme authority over man, this fanciful pattern of human conduct possesses the credibility of a superstition and is by common consent immune to the scientific tests of objective actuality.

"As to the variability and inconsistency of the standards of normality, examples are legion. We are supposedly a democratic country, but we are largely ruled by professional lobbyists. Overtly we support a war for world unification, but our ulterior intention leans strongly to the side of nationalism. In our commercial relations secret cartels often take precedence over our boasted policy of free enterprise. Everywhere codes of morality are juggled beyond recognition. Only a few years ago children stood in awe of their parents, now it is parents who stand in awe of their children. Divorce was formerly anathema, but today no stigma whatever attaches to it. One advocates democratic policies in his public life, but not infrequently adopts an attitude of imperialism in his home. Such will-o'-the-wisp principles of human behaviour and a thousand other catch-as-catch-can precepts are shared in varying forms by all peoples and bespeak once more the perennial imbalance and conflict, the vacillating factionalism and partitiveness that mark the habitual mode of adaptation we cherish as 'normality'."

Happily for the credit of Scottish intelligence today, the Earl of Lindsay is counterbalanced by the great Scottish dramatist, James Bridie, who boldly declares that Picasso is one of the outstanding geniuses in the world today and that if Picasso is not normal he would rather stand with Picasso than with all the hordes of the normal.

The stupidity of these diehard reactionary attacks on an

Raeburn: Macdonell of Glengarry
(*National Galleries of Scotland*)

Allan Ramsay: The Painter's Wife
(*National Galleries of Scotland*)

Robert Colquhoun: The Dubliners
(*Scottish National Gallery of Modern Art*)

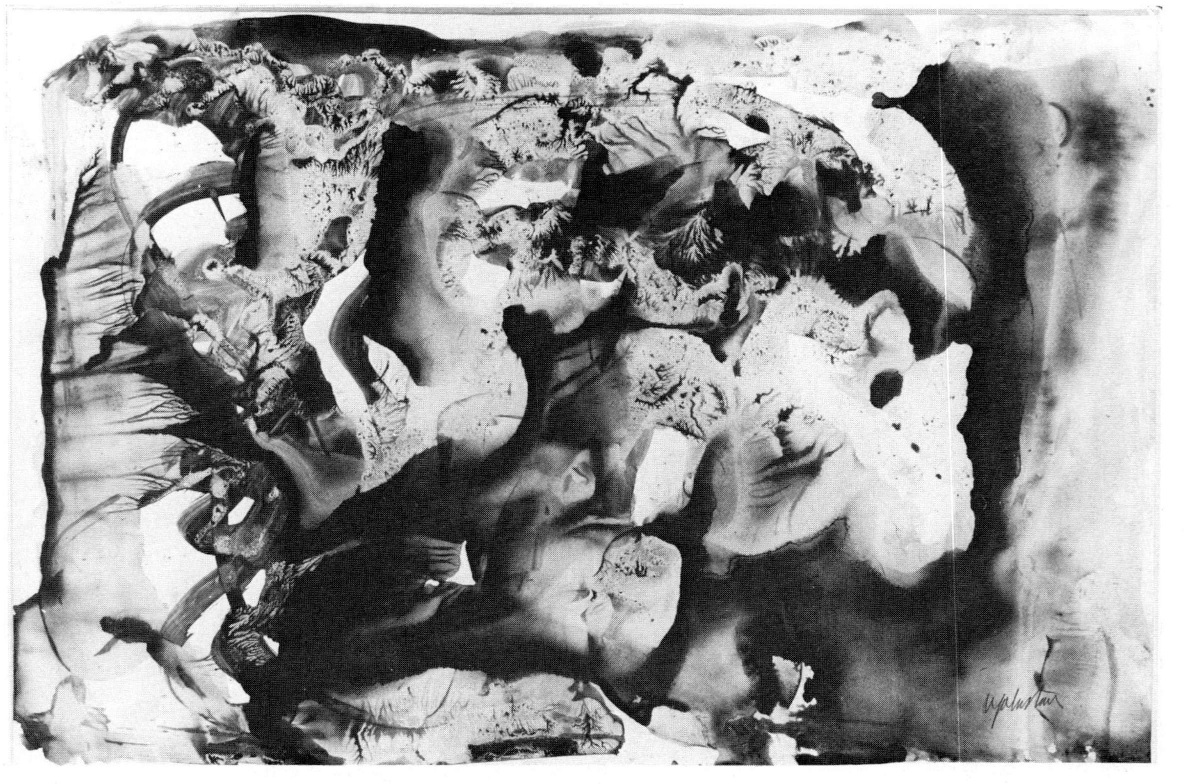

William Johnstone: Water Colour, 1931

(*Exhibited in the Mayor Gallery, London in 1933 or 1934*)

artist like Picasso, an author like James Joyce, and other leaders of modernist developments in the arts can best be appreciated when we reflect that Joyce's unrewarded attempt to establish the first motion-picture theatre in Ireland is only another chapter in the history of his misunderstandings with his country, but he fully understood the technical possibilities of the new medium. He keenly perceived—in spite of his defective vision—that the cinema is both a science and an art, and therefore the most characteristic expression of our time. Joyce's own technique shows the confluence of many modern developments in the arts and sciences. The impressionistic painters, by defining their object through the eyes of the beholder, gave Joyce an example which his physical handicap may have encouraged him to follow. The "ineluctable modality of the whole" was narrowed down for him, so that blurred sight looked for compensation in augmented sound. The Wagnerian school, with its thematic blend of music and ideas, had its obvious lesson for a novelist who had wanted to be a lyric poet or a professional singer. The international psychoanalytic movement, under the direction of Jung, had its headquarters in Zurich during the war years while Joyce was writing *Ulysses*, and he could scarcely have resisted its influence. And, although philosophy could not have offered him much in the way of immediate data, it is suggestive to note that Bergson, Whitehead, and others—by reducing things-in-themselves to a series of organic relations—were thinking in the same direction. Thus the very form of Joyce's book is an elusive and eclectic *Summa* of its age: the montage of the cinema, impressionism in painting, *leit-motif* in music, the free association of psychoanalysis, and vitalism in philosophy. Take of these elements all that is fusible, and perhaps more, and you have the style of *Ulysses*. To characterise this style, we must borrow a term from either German metaphysics or French rhetoric; we may conceive it as *Strom des Bewusstseins* or again as *monologue intérieur*. Of its prototype, Edward Dujardin's *Les lauriers sont coupés* it has been well observed that "it seems to bear the same relation to ordinary fiction that the film does to the stage. For, to find ample literary precedent for the internal monologue, we need only turn to the theatre. The conventions of Elizabethan drama permitted Shakespeare to marshal the arguments for and against suicide in Hamlet's soliloquy or to mingle desperation with prose and song in the distractions of Ophelia's madness. Recent playwrights, like Eugene O'Neill, have renewed their license to soliloquise. Poets like Browning and T. S. Eliot have never abandoned this prerogative."

Something very similar can be said of Picasso. But when Lord Lindsay attacks him in the name of normality, Lord Lindsay needs to be reminded of the queues at every picture-house and of the fact that the man-in-the-street and his wife—although they may jeer at and condemn a modernist picture or poem are at the very same time assimilating its techniques every time they go to the "movies" and are also taking it into their homes in the patterns of their new carpets and in the design of all sorts of other domestic gadgets.

The prejudice against modernist innovations is that of Lord Lindsay and other reactionaries; the general public have none of it. As Justice Brandeis said, "ordinary men and women can grasp the essentials of any situation, no matter how involved its details, if the facts are adequately presented to them." When the people of Mexico after the Revolution were given their first opportunity to hear the classics of European music at concerts in the public parks, it was not Bach and Mozart and Beethoven that evoked their enthusiasm but the most difficult atonal music of Schoenberg and his followers. It was with the dance as with music. Emmanuel Eisenberg reports that Anna Sokolow in introducing modern methods of choreography and novel dance technique for the first time into Mexico found that working-class pupils in that stronghold of folk-lore and ritual took to them readily and without any difficulty of adjustment.

It is exactly what the group of intellectual girls defying tradition and founding an association called Anggana Raras in Java with R. M. Kordat as leader have (again in dancing) done in another part of the world, influenced, as their spokesman R. Abdul Latief says, by what he calls "the new and young idea; back to your own culture, developing it in modern direction". That is the best possible advice for Scotland too, and is, in fact, exactly what the Scottish Renaissance Movement set out to do. The mass of the people will react all right if they get a chance. It is the stupid conservatism of their self-styled "betters" that is the danger. One sees easily enough why a great modernist poet and poetic dramatist like T. S. Eliot says that as far as his work is concerned he would prefer an audience of illiterates to an audience of half-educated conventionalists.

Another hang-over from the worst elements of the Common Sense Philosophy was represented by the plea put forward for amateurism by Sir Alexander Gray the other day. Sir Alexander denounced the radio, and the other modern facilities which have concentrated the arts more and more in the hands of professional artistes, and done away with the happy old times when far more people played an instrument in their own homes and associated with neighbours and friends in all kinds of humble social music-making. Whatever may be said of that from a merely human point of view, there can be no question that this development has been immensely to our artistic betterment. Vast numbers of people now hear first-class executants playing important music who would in former times—even as recently as fifty years ago—never have had any such opportunity. A vast amount of excellent instruction in appreciation of music and art and literature is constantly on the air. Amateurism has always been the curse of the arts in modern Scotland—amateurism, and, along with it, the inveterate predilection to "domesticate the issue". What Sir Alexander Gray recommends may suit the book of local exhibitionists, anxious to impress the neighbours, but the progress of the Arts in Scotland is dependent upon precisely the opposite course—upon, that is to say, the wider appreciation and striving after the highest possible standards.

Now in view of all I have said so far, it must surely come as a surprise when I have to go on to point out that in the article on Aesthetics in the 11th Edition of the *Encyclopaedia Brittanica*—after listing and discussing the great Greeks and the great Germans and French and others who have contributed importantly to this branch of philosophy and devised the various systems of aesthetics—we come to what are called the "English writers" on the subject—and find that thirteen of them are allotted separate paragraphs in which their contributions are described and assessed, and that of these thirteen no fewer than eight are Scots—namely, Francis Hutcheson, Thomas Reid, Sir William Hamilton, Lord Kames, Archibald Alison, Dugald Stewart, Alexander Bain, and John Ruskin. Not only so, but the text contains references to two other Scots, James Mill and Francis Jeffrey. Numerically at least that is an extraordinarily good proportion for Scotland compared with England in relation to a subject on which, I think, it would have been generally expected that Scotland would make a comparatively very meagre and miserable showing indeed. And on the strength of it I think I am justified in once again registering an emphatic protest at England's appropriation of Scottish writers in this way to hide or camouflage her own lamentable deficiencies. Not only are the Scots in the list more numerous; they are also more important—one of them, indeed, Ruskin, is as important as all the rest of the thirteen put together. Moreover the list is incomplete and excludes one important and far too little known Scottish writer, Aeneas Sweetland Dallas (1828–1879) of whose significance I must have a good deal to say before I finish. I am one of that very few and far between sort of Scotsman sufficiently interested in theories of art to look for and read all I can lay my hands on in this connection, and I may be allowed to reinforce what I have just said about the monstrous trick of describing Scottish writers as English by pointing out that in a recently-published massive volume in German, *Kunst und Literatur*, the writings of Engels and Marx dealing with the arts, I find that while Burns is properly described as a "schottischer Volksdichter" no less a person than Thomas Carlyle is listed as "englischer Schriftsteller", Sir William Hamilton as "englischer Philosoph der schottischen Schule", and John Stuart Mill as "englischer Philosoph und Okonom". The lines of Scottish thought and of the arts in Scotland have developed so differently from their English counterparts and point in such entirely different—

and, indeed, opposed—directions that it is important to clear up this kind of confusion and put these men all in their proper places in the traditions to which they really belong—and apart from which they cannot in fact be properly appraised at all.

I have pointed out elsewhere that any attempt to carry forward the Scottish philosophy—somewhat inaccurately called the Common Sense Philosophy—is discouraged by the Philosophy Professors of our universities and consequently little or nothing has been done about it in modern times. On the Continent, however—and in the United States of America—it has attracted some very able students and several important books on it have appeared there in recent years. For general reading, Dr. Henry Laurie's book, *Scottish Philosophy In Its National Development*, published in Glasgow in 1902, remains the best available. He devotes a chapter each to all the principal men—from Francis Hutcheson, Andrew Baxter, and David Hume, through Kames, Adam Smith, Thomas Reid, Dugald Stewart, and several others, down to Sir William Hamilton and James Frederick Ferrier. His phrase about "thoughtful minds occupied with philosophical questions in theological disguise" accurately describes most of the work of all these men. And, conveniently for our purpose, he has a separate chapter on 'Aesthetic Theories'. As he says, "the aesthetic theories favoured by writers of the Scottish school, from Hutcheson downward, are marked by a strong family likeness. They are almost unanimous in adopting a psychological method of inquiry, discussing the characteristics of our feeling of the beautiful and asking by what quality or qualities it is excited." He proceeds to discuss Hutcheson's essay 'Of The Standard Of Taste', Adam Smith's *Theory of Moral Sentiments*, Alexander Gerard's

'Essay on Taste', Dr. Hugh Blair's essay and Thomas Reid's and Lord Monboddo's and Dr. Archibald Alison's contributions to the subject, finishing up by considering Francis Jeffrey's 'Essay on Beauty', Dugald Stewart's *Philosophical Essays*, Thomas Brown's treatment of the Beautiful, and Sir William Hamilton's *Lectures*, remarking that for his theory of the sublime and beautiful Hamilton was indebted to Kant far more than to any of his Scottish predecessors (though he might have added that Kant himself was of Scottish descent). He sums up by remarking that "on the whole Scottish philosophy has been psychological in its treatment of these questions, its starting-point being the recognition of the emotion of the beautiful as a part of conscious experience, and its next step an enquiry into the source or sources of this peculiar emotion. This is still represented [he was writing in 1902] in some quarters as the only scientific method of inquiry. In the hands of the Scottish thinkers, at least, it did not lead to any triumphant success. From a psychological point of view, we are struck by the vagueness of the characterisation of the feeling of the beautiful. They were right no doubt in describing it as a pleasurable and disinterested emotion of a peculiar kind. But this did not carry them far into inquiring into its causes. It did not even relieve them from the ambiguity of the word beautiful, sometimes restricted in its application to nature and art, and sometimes extended to the world of mind. They were fortunate in lighting on the old conception of unity in multiplicity as a condition of beauty. But it was not till the influence of German philosophy began to be felt that an attempt was made to exhibit any rational connection between this condition and its effect. In the absence of such an explanation, they were naturally led to ask if the emotion of beauty might not be excited by a variety of external causes, or accounted for by a connected flow of ideas. Recent theories of Aesthetics have sought to surmount these difficulties by a more exact delimitation of the region of inquiry, concentrating attention more particularly on the Fine Arts. This, however, would have been impossible to Scottish writers in the eighteenth century. The tardy development of art in Scotland sufficiently explains the scantiness of their references to the nature, the history, and the masterpieces of music and the plastic arts, and even in literature the superficial judgment which preferred Corneille and Racine to Shakespeare [Dr. Laurie is referring here to certain notorious expressions of opinion made by David Hume] prevented their recognition of the catholic aims of art as the interpreter of nature and of human life in their fullest details and deepest meaning."

How far we have travelled since these vague explorations of "the feeling of the Beautiful", may be illustrated by quoting Dr. Herbert Read. "The concept of beauty," he says, "is, indeed, of limited historical significance. It arose in ancient Greece, and was the offspring of a particular philosophy of life. That philosophy was anthropomorphic in kind; it exalted all human values and saw in the gods nothing but man writ large. Art, as well as religion, was an idealisation of nature, and especially of man as the culminating point of the process of nature. The type of classical art is the Apollo Belvedere or the Aphrodite of Melos—perfect or ideal types of humanity, perfectly formed, perfectly proportioned, noble and serene; in one word, beautiful. This type of beauty was inherited by Rome, and revived at the Renaissance. We still live in the tradition of the Renaissance, and for us beauty is inevitably associated with the idealisation of a type of humanity evolved by an ancient people in a far land, remote from the actual conditions of our daily life. Perhaps as an ideal it is as good as any other; but we ought to realise that it is only one of several possible ideals. It differs from the Byzantine ideal, which was divine rather than human, intellectual and anti-vital, abstract. It differs from the Primitive ideal, which was perhaps no ideal at all, but rather a propitiation, an expression of fear in the face of a mysterious and implacable world. It differs also from the Oriental ideal, which is abstract too, non-human, metaphysical, yet instinctive rather than intellectual. But our habits of thought are so dependent on our outfit of words, that we try, often enough in vain, to force this one word 'beauty' into the service of all these ideals as expressed in art. If we are honest with ourselves, we are bound to feel guilty sooner or later of verbal distortion. A Greek Aphrodite, a Byzantine Madonna and a savage idol from New Guinea or the Ivory Coast cannot one and all belong to this classical concept of beauty. The latter, at least, if words are to have any precise meaning, we must confess to be unbeautiful or ugly. And yet, whether beautiful or ugly, all these objects may be legitimately described as works of art."

Mr. Eric Newton in his book on *The Meaning of Beauty* published the other day, stresses that the love of pictures has to be acquired with great patience. The only way of learning to enjoy pictures is to spend a lot of time looking at them and for most people this is impossible. Literature has been made easily available by printing, music by the gramophone and the radio; but painting remains difficult of access, for even the best coloured reproductions of a Titian or a Velasquez are no more faithful than old phonograph cylinders. "Art," says Mr. Newton, "is no more than the expression of human experience, and the understanding and enjoyment of art is no more than the capacity of the spectator to relate the work of art to his accumulated store of experience. It follows that the spectator's reaction to the work of art is limited by the scope of his experience. . . . Yet Human beings continue to quarrel among themselves about what is, or is not, beautiful, rather than about who is and who is not capable of recognising beauty."

"Such a distinction," Mr. Raymond Mortimer said in a review, "it will be said, is shockingly undemocratic: paintings ought to please the average man. But will even the most bigoted Marxist impose the same obligation upon chess-problems? By 'experience' Mr. Newton means not only study in museums but habitual responsiveness of eye in daily life. Most people use their sight very negligently except for an ulterior purpose such as to hit a ball, to avoid a fishbone, to appraise the expression, or the hat worn by a friend. The painter is continuously fascinated by appearances as such, by the mere look of everything—of slugs, of barbed wire, of old sardine-tins. So also is the lover of painting. This disinterested delight in shapes and colours can become one of the major rewards of living, but it is commonly sought only in things well-known to be beautiful—sunsets, for instance, and flowers and porcelain ornaments."

The reader who does not wish to read a book like Dr. Laurie's systematic philosophical exposition may find all he wants or needs about the earlier Scottish writers on aesthetics in J. H. Millar's *Literary History of Scotland* published a year later than Laurie's book, that is to say, in 1903. The book created a furore, evoking no little of that defense-reaction Dr. Trigant

Burrow describes in the passage I quoted dealing with normality. Dr. Millar was a wit and he exposed in a devastating way the absurdities and windy pretentiousness of much in the writings of the Scottish philosophers. He may be claimed by and large to have been the initiator of many of the leading ideas of the Scottish Renaissance Movement today and his most amusing attacks on the writers of the then popular Kailyaird School—Ian Maclaren, S. R. Crockett, J. M. Barrrie and others—struck pain and alarm into all the mindless sentimentalists round the parish pumps and bonnie briar bushes. Of Thomas Reid, he said: "Reid's philosophy has suffered to some extent from his employment of so ambiguous an expression as 'common-sense'. Passages like the following 'brust' of eloquence are not likely to restore confidence in that touchstone, or its champion:- 'Admired Philosophy! daughter of light! parent of wisdom and knowledge! if thou art she, surely thou has not yet arisen upon the human mind, nor blessed us with more of thy rays than are sufficient to shed a darkness visible upon the human faculties, and to disturb that repose and security which happier mortals enjoy, who never approached thine altar nor felt thine influence! But if, indeed thou hast not power to dispel those clouds and phantoms which thou hast discovered or created, withdraw this penurious and malignant ray; I despise Philosophy and renounce its guidance—let my soul dwell with Common Sense'."

Despite this ridiculous and all too typical flight of rhetoric, Dr. Millar recognised that there was a real core of substance in Reid all the same, and went on to say: "But, in making his appeal to Common Sense, Reid did not desire to take the judgment of the man in the street. He meant to appeal to those principles which are common to the understanding of all men, and which are the indispensable conditions precedent to an act of judgment on the part of any one."

More recent writers have tended to re-establish Reid as no unworthy antagonist of Hume himself—Hume of whom Sir Leslie Stephen said that the failure of English thinkers to face up to some of the problems posed by Hume, and by Hume alone, accounted for the pusillanimity and ineffectiveness of all subsequent English philosophy.

Of Sir William Hamilton's work, Dr. Millar says that many are now disposed to think his abilities were sadly wasted in wedding the philosophy of the unconditioned to the philosophy of "common-sense". Elsewhere Dr. Millar had said of Hamilton, "as a Professor he was a great success, commanding in all cases the attention and respect, and in not a few the enthusiastic devotion of his pupils. His favourite doctrines were championed by one of the ablest metaphysicians who adorned Oxford during the century, and denounced by one of the feeblest logicians that ever attempted to reason accurately. Yet now, there is scarce a Hamiltonian in the land. He is repudiated with zeal alike by empiricists and neo-Hegelians. His influence is imperceptible in modern thought; and there is no sign that the wheel of fashion will bring even a modified form of his system into vogue again. Wherein, then, lies the secret of the eclipse of this once brilliant luminary?" But I am not so sure that a measure of rehabilitation will not come to him even yet. I know that the late Lord-Tweedsmuir (John Buchan) was keen to attempt it. He told me that he had always cherished the hope of writing a study of Hamilton. His tremendous activities in other fields of literature and public life prevented him doing so. But the task may be discharged by some one else.

Of the other Scottish Philosophers Dr. Millar says enough to show that they owed most of what repute they had in their day to their fine presence and imposing personalities and gifts of eloquence, but that they added precious little of any value to the subjects on which they expatiated and have certainly little to yield to students of aesthetics today. Mr. A. D. Woozley's edition of Reid's *Essays on the Intellectual Powers of Man*, published in 1941, makes out a good case for Reid *vis-a-vis* Hume. And Dr. Norman Kemp Smith's book, *The Philosophy of David Hume*, a critical study of its origins and central doctrines, published in 1941, is a brilliant reassessment which does ample reparation to an ambiguous shade and marks the highest point of that apotheosis of Hume which had been proceeding throughout the previous decade. These studies, however, have little to do with our specific concern—that department of philosophy which is called aesthetics.[2] Nor is there much to our purpose in Mr. Jerome Hamilton Buckley's book, *The Victorian Temper* (1952), although it does introduce the reader to the now forgotten but once influential critical pronouncements of the Rev. George Gilfillan, and the much sounder achievement of David Ramsay Hay, who carried on the tradition of Kames and Alison by founding at Edinburgh in 1851 the Aesthetic Society, with the avowed object of discovering the objective principles which governed the creation of beauty.

It is very otherwise with A. S. Dallas, whose most important work, published in two volumes in 1866, bears the reassuring title of *The Gay Science*. Dallas was born in Jamaica in 1828. As a young man he studied Philosophy at Edinburgh, under Sir

William Hamilton, from whom he learned to apply psychology to the study of aesthetics. His first book, *Poetics, an essay in poetry* (1852) was a first draft for ideas which he developed fully in *The Gay Science*, but it has been remarked that it shows an acute and appreciative mind, scholarship, and a lively prose style, and is diversified with a wealth of anecdote, illustration, apt metaphor and shrewd incidental judgment. An article on criticism which he published in *The Times* revealed the same qualities, and Dallas became, and remained for many years, a member of *The Times* staff. He wrote fluently and accurately on politics, biography, criticism and other subjects. At the time of his death, in January 1879, he was preparing a new edition of the Maxims of La Rochefoucauld and his long essay on that subject is still unprinted. In addition to the two volumes of *The Gay Science* two others, dealing with the practical application of critical principles, were promised, but the first two were so poorly supported that the others were never written.

True criticism, Dallas contended, is threefold. It involves, first, the comparison of all the arts with one another, and a discussion of the common element which they are generally admitted to possess. Second, it involves a study of psychology, a comparison of all the arts with the nature of the mind, its intellectual structure, and its ethical needs. Third, it involves a comparison between the results thus obtained, and the facts of history, the influence of race, religion, and climate. "The great fault of criticism is its ignorance—at least its disregard—of psychology." Even Aristotle, for all his shrewd observation, provides no basis for a systematic criticism. "His leading principle, which makes all poetry, all art, an imitation, is demonstrably false, has rendered his Poetic one-sided (a treatise not so much on poetry as on dramatic poetry) and has transmitted to all after criticism a sort of hereditary squint." All ages have agreed that the aim of art is pleasure: the pleasure of imitation, said the Greeks. But the inadequacy of the Aristotelian conception was shown by the elder Scaliger: if all poetry is imitation, then prose is also imitation. The object of art is the pleasure of the beautiful, said the Germans; losing themselves in a cloud of transcendental tautologies. "The beautiful," says Hegel, "is the perfect expression of the perfect idea—my grand idea of the absolute, in which contraries are at one, and the all is nothing." The object of poetry is a pleasure of the Imagination, say English critics from Webbe to Johnson, using the word "imagination" vaguely and ambiguously. History, science and poetry, says Bacon, are the products of memory, reason and imagination respectively. But in the account of our faculties given by Locke, and almost every other English psychologist down to Herbert Spencer, the imagination is disregarded. "Imagination is the Proteus of the mind, and the despair of metaphysics." Addison uses the term merely to describe the power of visualising. The Germans pile confusion on confusion: Die Phantasie ist die Weltseele der Seele, und die Elementargeist der übrigen Kräfte. Coleridge is at his most portentous: "The imagination I consider either as primary or secondary. The primary imagination I hold to be the living power and prime agent of all human perception, and as a repetition in the finite mind of the eternal act of creation in the infinite I AM. The secondary I consider as an echo of the former."

"Oh gentle shepherds," cries Dallas, "What does this mean? It reminds me of a splendid definition of art which I once heard: when the infinite I AM beheld His work of creation, he said Thou Art, and Art was."

Dallas himself says that imagination or phantasy is a special function, not a special faculty, of the unconscious mind: "It is a name given to the automatic action of the mind or any of its faculties—to what may not unfitly be called the Hidden Soul." His object, he says, is not so much "to identify imagination with what may be called the hidden soul, as to show that there is a mental existence within us which may be so called—a secret flow of thought which is not less energetic than the conscious flow, an absent mind which haunts us like a ghost or a dream and is an essential part of our lives. Incidentally there will be no escaping the observation that this unconscious life of the mind—this hidden soul—bears a wonderful resemblance to the supposed features of imagination. . . . To lay bare the automatic or unconscious action of the mind is indeed to unfold a tale which outvies the romances of giants and ginns, wizards in their palaces and captives in the Domdaniel roots of the sea. . . . The hidden efficacy of our thoughts, their prodigious power of working underhand, can be compared only to the stories of our folk-lore, and chiefly to that of the lubber-friend who toils for us when we are asleep or when we are not looking."

The concept of the "unconscious mind" was not new; it had been recognised by Leibnitz, and in Germany the notion had already taken root and run to seed in the "absurdities and extravagances" of the transcendental philosophy. More recently it had been resuscitated in more measured terms by Sir William Hamilton, John Stuart Mill, and Herbert Spencer. Dallas, however, was making a definite contribution to the theory. He summarises the evidence for unconscious memory, and unconscious reasoning, but then adds: "There is in the mind, as I shall afterwards have to show, a genuine creative process, over and above the seeming creativeness of unconscious memory." Further he traces the relation of dreams and the unconscious: "The realities of our hidden life are best seen in the darkness of slumber." Indeed a *lack* of conscious effort seems to be necessary for the production of some works. "If you think how you are to write," said Mozart, "you will never write anything worth hearing."

Dallas did not, of course, completely forestall the psychoanalytic method: he did not explicitly enunciate the doctrines of transference and substitution; but he did see that the ways of the conscious mind can only be explained by assuming that it is sometimes fulfilling desires of which it is not aware, or is providing a substitute for those desires, and that the instincts often offer the plainest example of unconscious motives. He identifies the life of the unconscious mind with the inner life of the mystic as well as the inspiration of the poet.

"The great fact out of which it springs is the felt existence within us of an abounding inner life which transcends consciousness. We feel certain powers moving within us, we know not what; we know not why—instincts of our lower nature, intuitions of the higher, dreams and suggestions, dim guesses, and faint, far cries of the whole mind. There is a vast and manifold energy, spontaneously working in a manner which at once reminds us of Cuvier's definition of instinct as akin to somnambulism."

"All good poetry," says Dallas, "has a latency of meaning beyond the simple statement of facts," and the similarity of the arts lies in the fact that they act directly on the unconscious to produce an effect not wholly described or accounted for by the conscious thought which they arouse: the scientific "meaning" of Beethoven cannot be "compared" with that of Shakespeare. If we attempt to interpret music we are trying to produce through another medium effects in the hidden mind similar to those which were produced by the original. The pleasure which the artist aims at giving arises from "the quiet of the mind" but that quiet is not the quiet of inaction, but of harmony. Harmony itself may be indefinable, but we may nevertheless distinguish dynamic harmony and static. The former follows the contemplation of specifically dramatic effects, and corresponds to a mixed pleasure and a balance of conflicting emotions. As Dallas points out, we have no form of words which will rid us of this contradiction—that the contemplation and experience of pain may itself give rise to pleasure. Static harmony springs from the contemplation of things which are eternally and intrinsically beautiful: pure colours, straight and curved lines and the solids they generate, pure concords, and elegant theorems in mathematics, and all those objects whose absence is unfelt and painless but whose presence produces pleasure.

The effects of tragedy and comedy on the one hand, and "pure beauty" on the other, are both legitimate objects of the artist. But there is a third, which is concerned not with the harmony of the will or of the conscious mind, but with the hidden soul. This third type Dallas calls "the weird"; and the pleasure which it gives is neither the "mixed pleasure" of comedy or tragedy, nor the "pure pleasure" of impersonal beauty, but a specific excitement which is related directly to the hidden working of the mind, and is the essential mark of poetry and art. "You can," says Dallas, "have great art which is dramatic, you can have great art which is not beautiful, but you cannot have great art which is not weird."

This concern of art with the unconscious explains the relation of art and morality. Art, in so far as it is "weird", is not consciously concerned with morality. In art, as in religious ceremony, the symbolism and the effect upon the unconscious mind are the most important elements. Some critics have rated the activity of the conscious mind above all human values, and there are moralists who value a circumspect and conscious rectitude more highly than a natural and instinctive virtue. "The essence of life lies in thinking, and being conscious of one's soul," says Matthew Arnold, translating the French writer, Joubert. "In point of fact," Dallas replies, "it is out of a flourishing self-consciousness that suicide springs." It has been observed that there are moments, indeed, when Dallas seems an earlier and less harassed D. H. Lawrence, as when he speaks contemptuously of "the modern disease—excessive civilisation and overstrained consciousness". "Intense consciousness," he says, "is the all-in-all of philosophy; therefore philosophers think it must be the all-in-all of life." The method of Christianity, on the other hand, has often been to cherish impulse and to control the instinctive actions by the manipulations of the hidden soul; and, says Dallas, "Art is so far like the religion of the Gospel, that it is not satisfied with that righteousness which is of the law, and which is called virtue. It would fain put love instead of law, and the sense of delight for that of duty."

Poetry is thus the ethics of the unconscious. It operates

through fictions, ideas which would be false, or meaningless, or inaccurate for any purpose other than that for which they were put forward. Similarly, the lines and points of the mathematicians, and the legal fictions of the constitution, are inapplicable except within the framework for which they were devised. Poetry is essentially religious in temper, even when it shows some doubt of current dogma. "The poets whom we condemn for their scepticism," says Dallas, "saw before them but two types of theology—theology in the cold-blooded school of Paley, reduced to a system of clever contrivances, with springs and pulleys and most ingenious machinery; or theology in the more ardent school of the Wesleys and Whitefields, reduced to a system in which there was less of love and mercy than of hell and damnation. If thus in the earlier half of the century there flourished among us a mis-shapen theology, a clock-making theory of the universe which represented the Almighty as a sempiternal Sam Slick, hard of heart, but of infinite acuteness and softness of sawder, those are not wholly to be blamed who revolted against the creed because in their zeal they carried the revolt too far."

Dallas's signifiance can be best appreciated when his whole line of argument is set against Stanley Cursiter's bald statement (in his *Scottish Art*) that "Imagination has played only a small part in the art of Scotland. Portrait painters, landscape painters, painters of *genre* and of history, we have had in plenty, but works of real imagination have been few."

New life, Dallas contends, may have visited the Church, but the progress of the Church has been as nothing in comparison with the progress of the people. In the race between the press and pulpit, the pulpit has lost so much ground that it may even be said that the authors and journalists are now the true working clergy of the British Isles. Furthermore, "the development of literature in our day—the new power which we possess of acting on the masses and of being acted on—has led and is leading to many changes, but none more important than the withering of the individual as hero, the elevation and reinforcement of the individual as private man."

In art, it marks the culmination of a change which has been in progress from the time of Greece. "There was a time," says Dallas, "when we could draw a pretty clear line of demarcation between the private life and the public life—between private virtues and public virtues. Now the private virtues are becoming public, and the private life is rising into public importance. Publicity is the order of the day."

All this is influencing the intention and the method of the artist. "It is curious," says Dallas, "that at the very moment when we are proclaiming that party is dead, and that henceforth we must no more consider men, but measures, the biographical element predominates in our literature, and in public life the personal overrides almost every other consideration. We are not only deluged with biographies of all sorts and conditions of men, women, and children, from the pet parson to the pet pugilist, and from Mr. Brown's three wives to the sweet infant who was perfect in lollypops and Dr. Watts; we have biographies of horses, biographies of dogs, and everything is more or less regarded from the personal point of view."

To condemn these tendencies and struggle against them without tracing their causes is useless; but Dallas sees in them the symptoms of a widespread disease in the body politic. "There is," he says, "a pregnant saying of Goethe's . . . that thought widens but lames; that action narrows but quickens. The individual feels how thought cripples him; the nation feels how discussion cripples it; and we are keenly sensitive to the lameness thus produced."

In the reaction against excessive intellectualism there is a demand for violent sensation. Literature becomes the study of the abnormal. In reaction against the brutality of the new commercial system there is an idealisation of the weak and the incompetent; "in modern literature," as Dallas says, "we have the same phenomenon—the weak and the foolish made much of, and treated as of equal accounts with demigods . . . And so throughout the art of the day."

I agree with an anonymous essayist who says: "Against such disorder the work of Dallas stands as a dignified but ineffectual protest. He was concerned no less than modern writers with the relation of the individual and the mass, the life of the instincts and of the intellect, but he recognised that such critical work can take effect only when social conditions are in its favour and when it serves to crystallise opinions already widely but inarticulately held." The two volumes of *The Gay Science* produced little effect in their own time, but they are still worth reading. In some of his opinions Dallas had been forestalled—his theory of poetry is essentially that of Shelley, for whom poetry was "not subject to the control of the active powers of the mind"—but Dallas was remarkable not only for his outline of a psycho-analytic theory of art, but also for the acumen with which he observed and analysed the prevailing tendencies of his age. Finally, the anonymous essayist says: "It is not easy to judge the strongest undercurrents of our day, but in his obituary notices in *The Times* of Lord Minto, Metternich,

Macaulay, Thackeray, and Palmerston, Dallas looked further ahead than most men. He foresaw the problems of democracy; and like Macaulay, he feared the crises 'in which it may be necessary to sacrifice even liberty to save civilisation'." As a practical critic, as a metaphysician, as a student of immediate politics, he may have been less important than Matthew Arnold, Walter Bagehot, John Stuart Mill; but in principles of criticism, and in general insight into modern political tendencies, his work is no less acute than theirs, and no less valuable today.

It may have been thought that in what I have said of the obsolescence and humbug of Scottish philosophic writings I have implied that these can safely be disregarded now and need not be read. Nothing can be further from my contention. They must be read if only as a clue to thoughts and feelings still widely prevalent amongst our people although under a variety of disguises nowadays which may make it difficult to identify them with these earlier manifestations. Again careful study of them may help us from falling into similar traps. But above all with our new resources of interpretation we can also find fresh and useful meanings in much that taken in its conventional acceptation would be hopelessly out-of-date. Scottish artists have not written much. They have been unfortunately free from the habit of issuing manifestoes. Few of even the most interesting of them have been Boswellised at all. There are scanty records of their conversations. Yet it is surprising how much could be drawn from their autobiographies, biographies, letters, and occasional writings. That has yet to be done. In passing I will only give one or two illustrations of what may be come upon in even the most out-of-the-way quarters of our national literature. Sir R. G. Stapledon in his book on *Ley Farming* shows how the results of the most recent experimentation in this matter were anticipated long ago by Aberdeenshire farmers and refers to the valuable material to be found in books and articles written by these men and long lost sight of. In the same way discoveries are to be made in old literature in matters of art. At a time when there is a tendency to dismiss modernist artists with a jeering comment that they haven't even begun to learn how to draw properly and an insistence in many quarters on thorough training, it is, I think, useful, or at least entertaining to come across a description of a well-known artist's actual methods and to reflect that the slap-dash paint-pot-flinging ways ascribed to certain experimentalists today are by no means so new as is generally imagined. I cull the following from a little book entitled *Reminiscences of Eighty Years* by John Urie, published in Paisley in 1908. "It was about this time," he says, "that I first came into contact with Sam Bough, the famous artist. A great burly bearded fellow, speaking with a broad Lancashire accent, Sam was a rough diamond—but a diamond he was, and no mistake. There was nothing about him that was not genuine. When I first knew him he had just given up his job as a scene painter at the theatre, and was painting scenes and doing other pot-boiler work. But the mark of his genius was on all his pictures, and it was not long after this till his art brought him both fame and fortune. I had frequently seen Sam at the Garrick Club, sitting with a pint of beer and a long clay pipe, before I had the opportunity of speaking to him. Sam had been painting a panorama entitled 'The Overland Mail to India', which was to be exhibited in the City Hall. The man who was to run the show came to me and wanted me to prepare some wood engravings of the scenes for advertisement purposes. I asked him how I was to get them, and he told me to go along to a certain address in Bath Street and Mr. Bough would let me know how he wanted them done. I accordingly went up to the address and knocked at the half-open door. The big cheery voice of Sam bade me enter. On pushing the door open I saw the floor covered with a piece of canvas. The artist, with a pot of paint in one hand and a brush in the other, was walking over the canvas, giving a swish here and a splash there at what seemed a chaotic mass of paint. I said, 'I am afraid I will spoil your picture!' 'Not at all', he said, 'Come in; you will just give it a little extra effect!' I remember afterwards going to the City Hall to see that panorama, and being amazed at the wonderfully fine effect produced by what at close quarters seemed exceedingly rough work. Once when Sam Bough was painting a scene illustrating 'The Lady of the Lake' for the Theatre Royal, Mr. Glover came into the room. 'Sam, Sam, that won't do', he exclaimed. 'Won't it', answered Sam, 'Then how will this do?' and he dashed a pail of whitewash on the picture. Mr. Glover fled in hot haste but a few touches of Sam's deft brush turned the mass of whitewash into a foaming cataract. Sam Bough was a remarkably quick worker. I have seen him set up a number of pieces of cardboard, and then go round them, making a dash with his brush at each in succession. In this way he rapidly sketched at the same time half-a-dozen different pictures in less time than an ordinary man would have taken to paint one."

I was delighted the other day when I found a companion piece to that description of Mr. Urie's. It refers to the sardonic creations of Edward Burra, with particular reference to his picture 'Gorbals, Glasgow', painted years before Burra did his famous design for Arthur Bliss's ballet, *Miracle in the Gorbals*. The technique for these diabolical incantations, I learned, is simply to lie down on the floor with a pencil in your claw-like hand covering sheets of cartridge-paper with meticulous drawings which you afterwards reinforce, still on the floor, with water-colour. If the paper isn't big enough you simply pin the separate sheets together.

Whistler's mother, Anna MacNeill Whistler, was a Scotswoman, and in Elizabeth Mumford's biography of her, published in 1940, I was interested to come across the following passage which brings out so clearly the Gaelic spirit in her. "She had," says Miss Mumford, "a kind of aesthetic craving for perfection in her everyday life that came out in her son's passion for art in its purest essence; and if he arrived at his ideal by eliminating unessential detail, she approached hers by finding no detail unessential." As soon as I read that I recalled how John Tonge writing on 'Charles Rennie Mackintosh, Celtic Innovator', in *The Scottish Arts Review*, had remarked that "for most historians he is the master of *Jugendstil*, above all the *Innenarchitekt* who, agreeing with Muthesius that 'a room should be a work of art in itself, not the result of artistically worked pieces joined together', designed everything from the front door-handle to the contents of the cutlery canteen". While the genius of Mackintosh and his great influence on modernist developments in architecture have now been widely recognised, it is typical of the tremendous amount of study and critical examination that remains to be undertaken in every aspect of Scottish art—as in all other spheres of Scottish life—that his work raises big questions in certain directions which are far from settled. Mr. Thomas Howarth, who has recently lectured and broadcast a good deal on Mackintosh, sums up this divided character of his achievement when he says: "Mackintosh is now acclaimed a pioneer of the modern movement in architecture and the decorative arts. He remains, nevertheless, something of an enigma—the man largely responsible for an abortive outburst of *art nouveau*, a designer of tea-rooms and of absurdly high-backed chairs; and yet one who appears to have held in his hand the key to modern architecture."

In his range of reference and brilliance of unexpected but convincing analogies, and comparisons and cross references drawn from all the fields of human thought and activity, the ecological approach of which I have spoken—the taking in of all the connections between works of art and the thought, history, and phsyical features of a country—is shown by Mr. Ian Finlay as clearly as by Mr. Tonge. Mr. Finlay always considers a work of art in relation to the life and ideas of its time—and in relation, too, to the minor crafts. Examining Raeburn's 'Macdonell of Glengarry', for instance, he makes use of the fact that the pistols are English-made in order to emphasize the decline of Celtic Art after the Jacobite risings. He points out the connection between the Highland evictions and Horatio MacCulloch's grandiose landscapes, and between the creative vigour of Glasgow's industrialists and their support of the Glasgow School. There is a particularly brilliant juxtaposition of George Henry's 'Galloway Landscape' and the fifth-century Burghead Bull, with the same flowing rhythm perceptible in each.

Other contemporary Scottish writers who are doing the same sort of thing are Mr. Robert Melville, Mr. John Grierson in his writings on the documentary film and on the arts of the cinema in general, Mr. William Power in an interesting book in which he correlates Scottish literature and painting with the landscape—and when the restless and dynamic character of Scottish painting compared with English is being discussed it is certainly necessary to remember with Dr. Henry Meikle how sharp the transitions in Scottish scenery are, and what astonishing diversity our country packs into even the smallest regions.

It should always be borne in mind that while it is true, as a recent writer has said, that "twenty-five years after a book has been published is an awkward age, at which unintended 'period effects' begin to show themselves, and when ideas have been aired long enough for some of them to have gone bad", and most of the books of the Scottish aesthetic philosophers are much older than that, and have suffered far more from that kind of deterioration, so that only a very few elements in any of them retain any useful applicability today, it is also true that after such a passage of time they acquire other values in comparison with today's fashions in exposition, criticism, and taste, which may make them a useful corrective or standard of comparison. It is a very great mistake to allow an excessive contemporaneity to make us contemptuous of or indifferent to the very different standards of previous periods. There is also the fact—and this is especially true of a country like Scotland where the national tradition has been hopelessly fragmented or driven underground and very few people, if any, possess a complete knowledge of it, that the kind of reading I am recommending is likely to bring to light again all sorts of people of whom sight has been undeservedly lost and who ought to be kept in mind and esteemed at their true worth.

There is, for example, although his tribute is too highly-pitched, a great deal of truth in what Mr. Millar in his *Literary History of Scotland* says of a man of whom I suspect exceedingly few people today have ever heard at all, namely R. L. Stevenson's cousin, Robert Alan Mowbray Stevenson (1847–1900), the "Spring-heel'd Jack" of R. L. S.'s *Memories and Portraits*, and, *omnium consensu*, a master of the art of conversation. W. E. Henley's account of him, published in the *Pall Mall Magazine* of July, 1900, is well worth hunting out and reading. "Bob Stevenson," says Millar, "was anything rather than an easy or prolific writer. But when he did write, it was to some effect, for he wrote exclusively on the subject he knew best and had most at heart—pictorial and plastic art. An essay on Rubens, an all-too-brief treatise on *The Art of Velasquez*, published in 1895 and reprinted with some additions under the title of *Velasquez* in 1899, and the letterpress for Mr. Pennell's *Devils of Notre Dame* (1894) comprise the whole of his work that is accessible or that is not fragmentary. Yet small as is its bulk, its value is inestimable. The critic is never pugnacious or provocative; but what he conceives to be error is rebuked and refuted the more forcibly for the calmness and dignity of his manner. Here you feel instinctively is a man who really cares for painting *qua* painting, and not merely because he can connect it with some sentiment or anecdote or can deduce from it some moral lesson. To pass from Mr. Ruskin to Mr. Stevenson is to pass from thick darkness, illuminated by dazzling flashes of rhetoric, into the peaceful radiance of a summer's morning and a clear sky. What was revolutionary doctrine when Mr. Stevenson commenced critic is probably rigid orthodoxy now. Rarely do we hear Rembrandt or Rubens or Velasquez denounced as 'lost souls'. The tombs of the prophets have been piously ornamented by those who would have been the first to stone them; and the President of the Royal Academy is fain to admit that Alfred Stevens was an eminent sculptor. This may not mean very much; and the traditions of two or three generations are not easily subverted. But if the art-criticism of today is, upon the whole, more intelligent than the art criticism of twenty or thirty years ago—less dull, less perverse, less obstinately blind—it is perhaps to R. A. M. Stevenson more than to any other single man that the improvement, such as it is, must be ascribed."

A recent talk in the Third Programme by Mr. John Steegman on 'The Eastlakes and Lord Lindsay' recalled another Nineteenth Century Scotsman, who deserves to be given his place in such a survey, namely Lord Lindsay, who later became the 25th Earl of Crawford. As Mr. Steegman said: "He is one of the most important of the writers on art in the immediately pre-Ruskin generation, though he is hardly ever read today. Lindsay's great work was his three-volume *History of Christian Art* published in 1847. It is in fact a history of art from the early years of the Byzantine Empire, in the sixth century A.D. down to the High Renaissance. Calling it a history of *Christian* art was bound to excite controversy, at that particular time, and of course it did: there were attacks on it from the strictly Protestant historians such as Palgrave; from Ruskin to whom at that time the term 'Christian' inevitably implied a hatred of Rome; from those who regarded Renaissance Art as Pagan and not Christian at all; and from those who regarded pre-Renaissance art as merely barbarous. The work, however, was widely accepted as the great achievement which it undoubtedly was. To use it reveals Lindsay as being in the small advance-guard of critics beginning to understand and love the Early Masters. When he stated, for instance, that the fountain-head of all Florentine art was Giotto, he effected a revolution in criticism by putting back that source from its previously accepted place at the end of the fifteenth century to the end of the thirteenth. In another direction Lindsay took a far more seriously considered view of Byzantine art and civilisation than was then generally held." Reference should also be made here to another great Scottish virtuoso—Sir William Stirling Maxwell (1818–1878) whose works, including *Annals of the Artists of Spain*, published in 1848, and whose collection, including works by El Greco and Blake, is still to be found in Pollok House.

In another Third Programme talk, on Palladianism in England, this time by Professor Wittkower, the Durning-Lawrence Professor in the History of Art at London University, we were reminded of two other Scots of whom perhaps we know too little. "The genesis of this eighteenth-century Palladianism is well known to us," said Professor Wittkower. "The crucial year was 1715. In that year appeared in London the first volume of Colin Campbell's *Vitruvius Britannicus* as well as the first instalment of Giacomo Leoni's English edition of Palladio's book on architecture. In their prefaces both Campbell and Leoni pay tribute to the genius of Palladio. Campbell attacked the licentiousness and extravagance of the Italian baroque and singled out the great Palladio who has exceeded all that were gone before him and surpassed his contemporaries. And indeed," he continues, "this excellent Architect seems to have arrived at a *ne plus ultra* of his art. With him the great

Manner and exquisite Taste of Building is lost." Colin Campbell went from Scotland to London, perhaps in 1712 or 1713. His age, as well as his Scottish beginnings are shrouded in mystery, but Professor Wittkower adduces facts to show that the old and often repeated legend of Lord Burlington as patron of Campbell's work as well as Leoni's must be dismissed. "Burlington House was the first building of the new style in London. It opens an architectural era which, one can safely say, changed the face of England. But in spite of careful research into the history of Burlington House, some questions have so far evaded solution. The mention of the rebuilding in Gay's *Trivia* is proof that the new structure was well under way in 1715. The architect in charge was James Gibb—another Scotsman, an Aberdonian who had studied under Fontana in Rome, and who designed St. Mary-le-Strand, St. Peter's Vere St., and St. Martin-in-the-Fields; part of the Senate House and of King's College, Cambridge; the monuments of Ben Jonson, Prior, and Newcastle in Westminster Abbey; the quadrangle of St. Bartholomew's Hospital, and the Radcliffe Library, Oxford, as well as publishing several books on architecture and translating foreign books on the subject. Gibb however did not proceed very far with Burlington House. It would appear that Burlington first took him on as the architect who had the best Italian schooling and who, having recently returned from Italy (in 1709) after a long stay in Rome, would build for him something thoroughly Italian. But after the publication of the first volume of *Vitruvius Britannicus*, the Earl, suddenly converted to Palladianism, switched over to Campbell, leaving only the execution of the forecourt in Gibb's hands. Colin Campbell erected some of the most important neo-Palladian buildings between 1715 and his premature death in 1729. His first great country house commission was Wanstead House, built between 1715 and 1720, and demolished in 1822. The commission from the Prime Minister, Sir Robert Walpole, for Houghton followed in 1722. From Houghton onwards the most important country house commissions went to the Burlingtonians. Campbell himself built Mereworth Castle in Kent between 1723 and 1725 in close analogy to Palladio's celebrated Villa Rotonda. When the second half of the century opened most architects of the Burlington group were dead or in retirement. The stars of William Chambers and Robert Adam (two other Scots whose names remain better known) were rising, and neo-Palladianism as an architectural style was succeeded by neo-Roman, neo-Greek, and neo-Gothic tendencies."

I would also mention the French philosopher, Professor Denis Saurat's article 'Scottish Intellectualism: William Johnstone' which appeared in *The Studio* of August, 1943 and discussed the work and ideas of Mr. Johnstone, a Scottish artist, who has published two books, *Creative Art In England* and *Child Art to Man Art*. Since Scotland lacks a centre and shows no thrift in dealing with its men of talent but disperses them to the ends of the earth and fails to claim them and build their achievements into the records of our national accomplishment, it is excessively difficult to get an all-in view. I imagine that it will come as a surprise, for example, to be reminded that Lady Mendl—Miss Elsie de Wolfe—the great international de luxe decorator of millionaires' mansions had a Scottish mother, Georgina Copeland, the daughter of a chaplain at Balmoral. "One of the last big American places she decorated was Gary Cooper's at Brentwood, California. Here the Elsie-de-Wolfe—

Lady Mendl modern style is as recognisable as a signature, with its dramatic use of black and white, Zebra skins, Venetian starred mirrors, and its cardinal colours in upholstery against near-white walls or near-white upholstery against coloured walls. In the summer of 1936 she came again into the decorating news when it was reported that she was about to modernise Buckingham Palace for King Edward VIII. This she denied, stating that she had merely executed models, which had pleased His Majesty, for the redecoration of three rooms at Fort Belvedere. The official entertaining by Sir Charles and Lady Mendl is done in her Paris flat on the Avenue d'Iena, which is a sumptuous formal residence. Its salon is decorated with fine pieces of the French haute epoque. There are excellent boiseries throughout; chairs, signed by Cressent, covered with 16th century blue velvet, and a small highly personal collection of 18th Century *grisailles* and wash drawings by Boucher, Watteau, Fragonard and Carmontelle. Her Villa Trianon, however, is her real pride. Its property deed, dated 1750, deserves a right-of-way for all time for the King of France. Lady Mendl spent thirty years and a considerable fortune restoring the place, which had formerly belonged to King Louis-Philippe's son, the Duc de Nemours and she made it a model of perfection in period furnishings, terraces, gardens, and the landscape perspectives so precious to the old French ideal. The Savonnerie carpets, the Louis XV marquetry, General Murat's iron camp bed, a Clodion nymph and faun, and copies of the famous Mille Graces curtains (whose originals she possessed till they dropped to dust) are some of the house treasures. I should not be surprised to learn that Miss Elsa Maxwell is half-Scottish too."

William McCance: From another window in Thrums
(1928)

Robert Crozier: Men in Pub
(*1971*)

John Bellany: Self-Portrait with Owl Mask
(*1974*)

Alexander Moffat: Summer Evening 1974

I would like to refer also before I close to Sir Eric MacLagan's Memorial Service tribute to D. S. MacColl, 1858–1948. "As of Browning's poet," said Sir Eric, "it may truly be claimed that MacColl lived 'through a whole campaign of the world's life and death'. Never has a man plunged with greater gusto into controversy. London is dotted with his battlefields—St. Paul's, Westminster Abbey, the Royal Academy, the Tate Gallery, Waterloo Bridge—not all of them, alas!, scenes of victory. And his opponents, even when they were skilled masters of fence like Roger Fry, could hardly have denied that his sword was as formidable as his nose. He often fought on the friendliest of terms; I remember him saying to me some twenty-five years ago, when he proposed to attack an acquisition of which I think we were justly proud at the Victoria and Albert Museum: 'You won't mind my alluding to your new bust as an unclean bird's nest.' But his convictions were theologically adamantine; he was not a son of the manse for nothing, though he carried his passionate orthodoxy and his heresy-hunting into another field. On some subjects, such as English prosody, he would hardly admit that anyone else was to be saved; like the legendary Scottish lady, he had his doubts about John. 'MacColl, you're too didactic', were the last words his friend Tonks spoke to him—indeed he is said to have expressed himself more strongly still, viz 'If MacColl met God Almighty, he would criticise Him to His face'. Generous as his admirations were, criticism was certainly his first instinctive reaction, and it was with pardonable exaggeration that Robbie Ross once suggested: 'MacColl loves art so much that he hates all works of art'. Yet when he did applaud he applauded with his whole-heart, and it is now fifty years since the great Glasgow

Exhibition of 1900 gave him the opportunity to open the eyes of a whole generation, to the glories of the French Impressionist School. We remember him for such characteristics as these; but we remember him too as a painter whose sensitive water-colours won the praise of artists whom he acknowledged as his betters—and that was the praise he really cared to win; as a poet, ranging from the uproariously comic to grave and solemn harmonies that were all his own; as a critic whose main fault was that he wrote far too little. We remember him as the head of two great London galleries, a colleague whose work was an inspiration to many younger men; and as one who played no small part in the creation of the New English Art Club and the National Art Collections Fund and the Contemporary Art Society. But most of all we remember him here as a friend; friend of many great men who have gone before him into another world, and of whom he had so much to tell us, Beardsley and Conder and Bob Stevenson, York Powell and W. P. Ker and Oliver Elton, and in a later vintage Tonks and Rothenstein and Wilson Steer . . . It is that larger assembly of the dead whom MacColl himself has now joined, the last, one would say, of a mighty generation, his own life prolonged beyond any normal span of years. . . . And he has left us too his message. In the words with which only a year or two ago he concluded his book on Wilson Steer: 'The battles of Beauty are never finally won; in each generation they must be fought afresh; it depends upon a few voices in each of them whether Titian counts as a master. Let us not be missing among "Knights of the Holy Ghost".' From the roll of that order the name of Dugald Sutherland MacColl is not absent; in it he lived and fought and died; may he rest in peace."

Another implacable fighter whose autobiography and correspondence—both of which he was preparing for publication before he died—was the sculptor, James Pittendrigh MacGillivray, whose colleagues in the Glasgow School had good reason to distort his surname into MacDevilry! I do not know what happened to his papers, but he figured in many famous rows, and compiled racy accounts of them. I hope they may yet be published, and add another notable volume to the all-too-few records of the sort that have been penned by Scottish artists—a companion volume, by a man of very different temper, to Sir John Lavery's autobiography, *The Life of a Painter*, published in 1940, and telling of his Glasgow days, when he was without board or lodging, sleeping on benches in Glasgow Green, picking up food that had been thrown away, and washing in the fountains when daylight came.

In conclusion, I want to say that I agree with Herbert Read when he says: "It is the practical men of affairs who have solved the problems of art. It is the engineers who built the Forth Bridge and the Crystal Palace, who have more recently evolved the form of the automobile and the aeroplane, who first unconsciously suggested the elements of a new aesthetic . . . a new tradition, based on practical realities, was formed." In commenting on this Mr. Ian Finlay quotes something I wrote over 20 years ago, as follows: "What has taken place in Scotland up to the present is that our best constructive minds have taken up engineering and only sentimentalists have practised art. We are largely (the world has assessed us rightly) a nation of engineers. Let us realise that a man may still be an engineer and yet concerned with a picture conceived purely as a kind of engine which has a different kind of functional power to an engine in the ordinary sense of the term. Here then is what we Scots have—a terrific vitality combined with a constructive ability unequalled by any other nation. What more do we need?—merely sufficient analytical power to clear away the maze of sentimentality and accepted 'artistic' values which obscure our ideas of Art."

All the things by which Scotland has captured the world without losing its own soul, have been its most indigenous, exclusive and inimitable things. I mean on different levels such things as Scotch whisky, our tartans, our traditional Scottish dances, and our pipe-music. True some of these are still inadequately or wrongly appreciated. Piping, for instance, not only amongst foreigners, but amongst most of our own people knowledge of piping is limited to strathspeys and military marches and to "smart fingering" and far too little is known of one of the greatest glories of Scotland, the *Piobaireachd*. All that means is that there is in these matters room to grow—room for creative developments, better informed appreciation, and fundamental exposition.

I mention the value of these peculiarly native things which carry both the credit and the cash—they are among our greatest dollar earners—not only for that reason, but because I do not think there can be any better description of any work of very high artistic value in any medium than just to be able to say of it with truth that it is *mar a tha e* as good whisky is—a Gaelic phrase meaning not only neat, clear-run, pure, or, in Rainer Maria Rilke's words, "filled with itself alone", but meaning all that is meant by achieving artistic unity. It is, however, in another homely illustration here in Glasgow with its great tradition of shipbuilding that I think I can come still closer to a definition of what we mean by art and should strive for and look for in all creative productions submitted to our judgment. No one has ever been able satisfactorily to explain—probably no one ever will be—the exact nature of that subtle process by which some man-made structure of iron, wood, or steel, is changed from a mere mass of inanimate and unresponsive matter into a thing with a character, a disposition, almost a personality of its own. Yet that some such transformation does sometimes occur cannot be denied explanation apart—most frequently, perhaps, where its subject is a ship. More than one notable instance come readily enough to the mind. The Cutty Sark had that quality of personality. The Thermopylae had it. The Mauretania—for it is by no means confined to sailing craft—had it, while the Lusitania had not, though they were like as two peas from one pod. The Queen Mary probably has it, though she has not yet had quite time enough to prove it in her sea-going career. And in her own particular class the King's Britannia—as her skipper, Commander Irving, aptly termed the famous old cutter in the book he wrote about it—possessed it as possibly no other yacht, large or small, has ever done. Of course in large part she owed her popularity, a popularity which extended far beyond the ranks of those usually interested in the technicalities of yacht design and racing, to her Royal ownership. But that by no means accounts for the quality with which I am concerned. One July day in 1936, forty-three years after she left the Clyde waters whence so many of the great "personality" ships, both sail and steam, have come, she was launched once more from the ways at Cowes for the last time. "Requiescat Britannia! Your memory will live". Assuredly the remembrance of the great old cutter is one which a far wider world than the inner circles of yachting will not willingly let die. Just that capacity for a man's work to leave his hands and sustain a "life" of its own is what is required of anything that deserves the name of a work of art, and if we Scots can achieve it in shipbuilding and engineering, we ought to be able with a very slight alteration of the direction of our energies, just the matter of putting the emphasis in a different quarter, to do it in painting and sculpture too.

The Scottish dichotomy between experience and consciousness—the dissociation in our midst between energy and sensibility, between conduct and theories of conduct, between life conceived as an opportunity and life conceived as a discipline—cannot be healed in the Edinburgh Festival way. Our national culture suffers from all the ills of split personality. The Edinburgh Festival's high prices excluding most of our people, together with its importation of foreign arts and artists and the virtual exclusion of our own, simply accentuate this schizophrenia. The dissociation of mind from experience in our midst has resulted in truncated works of art, works that tend to be either naive and ungraded, often flat, reproductions of life, or else products of cultivation that remain abstract because they fall short on evidence drawn from the sensuous and material world. It would seem now that some of our better-off people, in compensation for backward cultural conditions and a lost religious ethic, are developing or pretending to develop through this Festival a supreme talent for refinement just as a certain type of Jew, in compensation for adverse social conditions and a lost national independence, developed a supreme talent for cleverness. The one must inevitably be as flashy and meretricious as the other has been. This peculiar excess of refinement is bad in these Edinburgh Festival patrons, and not to be equated with the refinement of artists like Proust and Thomas Mann, as in the latter it is not—as it is in the former—an element contradicting an open and bold confrontation of reality. The explanation of the commodity-fetishistic attitude behind these Festival programmes is not difficult to discern. Artemus Ward wrote that "the Tower of London is very popular with people from the agricultural districts". In the same way the Edinburgh Festival is very popular with our cultural provincials. Its borrowed plumes are designed to dazzle our wealthier yokels.

In what I have said of engineering and the possibility of a redirection of our principal aptitudes into modern artistic channels lies perhaps our best chance of development today. However that may be, let me summarize the actual aesthetic position of Scotland up to the present date. The distressing thing about the early Scottish aestheticians has been their poor fruits. Their immediate successors were more arbiters of good taste than philosophers. As philosophy in Scotland came more and more to mean only Moral Philosophy, the divorce between artist and thinker became more complete than ever, and when the revival of aesthetic studies came on the Continent Scotland had no equivalent, however small, of Baudelaire, Hanslick, or even Pater. From the consequences of that we still suffer.

The Scottish artist has had little time for aesthetics, sometimes to his advantage sometimes not. There is the letter Sir Walter Scott wrote to the Duke of Buccleuch when asked to look over some paintings belonging to Stuart of Dunearn. After studying the most important, Hobbema's 'Avenue at

Middelharnis', Scott decided it was "fitter for an artist's studio than a nobleman's collection. Your Grace may be reconciled to it by the figure of a shooter and a Spanish pointer who are coming down the road in quest of water-fowl. It is the last thing I would buy for my own taste."

In the practice of the arts, the Scot has tended to eschew aesthetic theories, has usually been content to be a traditionalist like Burns, and always at his best has been a realist. Theories of painting up to a century ago hardly affected Scottish painting. John Pope-Hennesay said at the time of the Burlington House Exhibition of Scottish Art (1938) that of the 550-odd paintings in the Exhibition "a bare dozen make any predominantly aesthetic appeal", but by "its healthy philistinism" Scottish painting "had escaped the hideous falsity of much English painting". Realism, in that statement, would have been a better word than "philistinism". The achievements of Scottish painting have all owed much to realism—Geddes's grand portraits, Ramsay at his best (his prettinesses have blinded people to his asperities), the wonderful intimacy with his sitters that enabled Raeburn (so little an aesthetic painter compared to Reynolds) to overcome great technical shortcomings, the brand of impressionism to which McTaggart came by way of realism. On the other hand, the Italianate classicisers of the 18th Century and the romanticisers of the 19th (such as the pathetically Anglicised Wilkie) never pulled their proper weight.

This realistic tradition of the Scot is obscured when Scottish art is considered as part of English art (as when Lord David Cecil recently ranked Scott as a great historical novelist and then proceeded to praise him above all for characters like Jeannie Deans and Edie the old beggar, who to Scott were not history but real people!). This realism has, of course, often, too often, become mere matter-of-factness, incapable of being a vehicle of the imagination, of rising to heights of realistic fantasy. And when Scottish painting became aesthetic, the Glasgow painters, rebelling against the matter-of-factness and its complementary sentimentality, fell for mere decoration. Now MacBryde and Colquhoun have won through Cubism to a new realism combined with deep emotional content and in this way can be reckoned traditionalists.

This takes us far enough away from the Scottish aestheticians who are my concern. It would require careful research to determine to what extent the Rule of Taste that prevailed by the time of Blair and Christopher North was, like other rules of the time, English rule. The philosophical movement that produced Hume's 'Of the Standard of Taste', Alison's 'On the Nature of Taste' and so on sprang from much deeper sources than the latter-day good taste of the bourgeoisie. ("On the credit side, no good taste is anywhere discernible," said Wyndham Lewis of Léger the other week.) It is to Hume, of course, that most importance must be attached. The decline within the next century was catastrophie. Just as philosophic poverty is reflected in Scottish political thinking, the neglect of aesthetic studies is evident every day in what passes in Scotland for criticism. How many averagely-educated Scots can speak intelligently (as a Frenchman might) of, say, the differences between Celtic art and post-Reformation art, between the Old Town of Edinburgh and the New, between the ballad of Gil Morrice and the *Douglas* Home derived from it, between a pibroch and a hymn, between an English pre-Raphaelite and a Scottish genre-painter.

It's not just an academic issue. Clearly, for example, political and other expediencies determine that James Bridie and Eric Linklater will be produced at the Edinburgh Festival, instead of Ewan MacColl and Robert McLellan; but how have the pundits decided on Home's *Douglas*? In the past day or two I've heard the play dismissed as trash and praised to the skies, but not a single comment indicating a real awareness of its kind, its excellence or otherwise of its kind, the place of its kind in Scottish literature, and the desirability of considering carefully what future that kind can and should have in comparison with other kinds in relation to the future of Scottish drama.[3]

Since the above was written there have been considerable developments in the arts in Scotland, but few of these have been Scottish and most of them negative.[4] By the last-named I mean that recrudescence of philistinism that has characterised public discussion of the Edinburgh Festival programmes, and to a considerable extent also public criticism of sound radio and TV programmes—almost always opposed in the crudest way to new and experimental work, and dominated by the vociferations of purblind members of the Moral Rearmament Movement. In all of this little indigenous Scottish work has been involved—though developments of abstract painting have shared in this orgy of vicious disapproval. The establishment of a Gallery of Modern Art in the Botanic Gardens, Edinburgh, has hardly helped matters, since the Scottish element included is extremely small. There has nowhere yet been a thorough cleansing of the Augean Stables, and the appearance in the Scottish Press and other quarters of new writers on Aesthetics, concerned with the Scottish position in the arts, has so far been very sporadic and partial. Even an admirable innovation like the Traverse Theatre Club in Edinburgh has relied mainly on kinds of work not yet—or ever likely to be—naturalised in Scotland; the folk-song movement is bogged down in senseless repetition and a hopelessly sentimental attitude to an irrecoverable past, and only occasionally shows signs of coming alive in our own time and addressing itself effectively to current issues, as in some of the admirable anti-Polaris songs of Thurso Berwick and his friends, and the earlier achievements of like kind occasioned by the Coronation Stone episode. In the articles of *The Scotsman* drama critic, Mr. Ronald Mavor (son of the dramatist, "James Bridie"), in the propaganda for realism of Alan Bold and his artist friends in *Rocket*, in the continued writings of William Johnstone and William McCance, there are signs of a genuine advance, but these are still very fragmentary and of little effect in offsetting the general Philistinism. Worst of all is the continued absence of competent modern philosophising in Scotland, and above all the absence of aesthetic thought of any such value as might realign Scotland with other Western European countries and induce aesthetic developments based on Scottish roots and yet able to withstand comparison with the contemporary aesthetic thought of other countries. The omens are not auspicious. All we can hope for, it would seem, is, as in the past, an occasional voice crying in the wilderness, while the increased facilities given by the great increase of public leisure and affluence, the easier access of foreign arts of all kinds, the work of the Scottish Committee of the Arts Council and of the BBC and BBC-TV in Scotland lead only to a monstrous babble of incompetence as in the 'Arts Review' feature of the Scottish Home Service of the BBC and to only a slightly less appalling state of affairs in the 'Scottish Life and Letters' Programmes of the same body.

NOTES

1 Hugh MacDiarmid, *Lucky Poet*, London 1943, pp. 375–6.
2 In the 1970 TS the paragraph ends at this point. The concluding sentence—from "Nor is there" to "the creation of beauty"—was added later, probably in 1952 when MacDiarmid came across the Buckley book he cites.
3 In the 1950 TS this paragraph ends on a slightly different note, viz: "In the past day or two I've heard the play dismissed as trash and praised to the skies, but not a single comment indicating a real awareness of its kind, its excellence or otherwise of its kind, the place of its kind in Scottish literature, and the desirability or otherwise of encouraging that kind. We are a breed of critical simpletons." At this point the 1950 TS ends.
4 This—from "Since the above was written" to "most of them negative"—is the first sentence of the additional paragraph written probably in 1965. At that time the present editor was producing the broadsheet *Rocket*, mentioned in the new conclusion, and MacDiarmid (who contributed occasionally to the broadsheet) was in sympathy with the editorial line which promoted the figurative art (of, for example, John Bellany) as the most appropriate pictorial idiom for Scotland. Other contributors to *Rocket* included the painters Robert Crozier and Alexander Moffat.

Index

Index